THE VALENTINE
BRIDE

THE VALENTINE BRIDE

BY

LIZ FIELDING

MILLS & BOON®

First published in Great Britain 2006
Large Print edition 2007
Harlequin Mills & Boon Limited,
Eton House, 18-24 Paradise Road,
Richmond, Surrey TW9 1SR

© Harlequin Books S.A. 2006
Special thanks and acknowledgement are
given to Liz Fielding for her contribution to
The Brides of Bella Lucia series.

ISBN-13: 978 0 263 19460 9

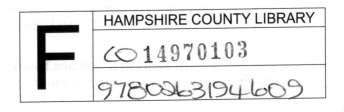

This book is for my daughter, Amy;
the joy of my life, my dearest friend, she
fills my head with stories and
never fails to make me laugh.

CHAPTER ONE

'I'VE printed out the PR schedule for this week's lead-up to the re-launch. The *City Lights* tie-in—' Louise Valentine broke off as her cell phone began to burble. 'I'll have to take this,' she said, excusing herself from the Nash Group executives gathered around the conference table for her briefing. 'I'm expecting a call from the editor…'

But as she flipped open the phone the caller ID warned her that it wasn't editor of the country's major 'scene' magazine.

It was Max.

For a moment she couldn't think, couldn't move, but then he'd always had that effect on her. Reducing her to a quivering wreck with a look that suggested it was a toss up whether he kissed her or strangled her. Since kissing her wasn't an option, she'd made a point of keeping her distance other than at family gatherings. Even then, by mutual consent, they'd chosen opposite ends of the room.

Unfortunately that was no longer a choice for

either of them, but clearly Max was as unhappy about that as she was. He had certainly taken his time about making a moment in his busy schedule to talk to her about taking on marketing and publicity for the Bella Lucia restaurant group now that he was in charge.

Well, too bad. Her schedule was busy, too. She wasn't sitting around waiting for the phone to ring. On the contrary, the phone never stopped ringing. She was in demand, a success in her own right.

She hadn't looked back since the day he'd fired her from the family business, leaving her in no doubt that, far from being an asset to Bella Lucia, as far as he was concerned she was nothing but a liability.

Okay, she'd be kidding herself if she didn't admit that there had been moments in the last couple of weeks when she'd found herself doodling ideas on her jotter, daydreaming about what she'd do if she did take on PR and marketing of the Bella Lucia restaurants; the fact that it would mean working with Max never failed to tip the dream over the edge into nightmare territory.

Even now he was only calling her because he'd had his arm twisted; she knew he'd have refused point blank to consider it if the suggestion had come from anyone but Jack. Max's half-brother might not have wanted to stick around and run the company himself, but as he was a major investor his suggestions carried the kind of weight that not even Max could ignore.

So far Max hadn't been able to find the time to pick up the phone and ask her if she was interested in the job, forget actually getting to the point of sitting down and talking the future through with her. Hadn't done one thing to make her feel she was needed, that her ideas would be welcome, let alone valued. Well, why would he? She wasn't a genuine Valentine—

'Louise?'

She glanced up, realised that everyone was waiting. She snapped the phone shut, turned it off, tried to recall where she'd been in her briefing. *City Lights...*

'As you know, *City Lights* ran the offer for a limited number of complimentary tickets to the opening of your London flagship restaurant in today's issue. Free food, live music and the opportunity to mingle with celebrities; a chance to live the aspirational lifestyle for a night.' She looked up. 'You'll be gratified to learn that the response was so great that it crashed the *City Lights* systems, a story that was reported in the later editions of the London evening papers and will run in the diary columns of tomorrow's dailies.'

'Well done, Louise,' Oliver Nash said. 'With luck the tickets will be changing hands on eBay for hard cash by this time tomorrow.'

'If they are,' she replied, matter-of-factly, 'luck will have had nothing to do with it.'

Max heard the voicemail prompt click in, then Louise's cool, businesslike voice suggesting he leave a message, assuring him that she would return his call as soon as possible.

That would be about as likely as a cold day in hell, he thought, ignoring the invitation and tossing the phone onto his desk. Why would Louise bother to call him back? Why would she waste one moment of her time doing what he wanted? It had been years but she'd never forgotten, or forgiven him for firing her.

As if he'd had any choice.

One of them had had to go and Bella Lucia was his future, the one fixed point in his life. Even when his father had been changing wives faster than most men changed cars. When his mother had been more interested in her career, her lovers.

Everyone knew that Louise was just filling in time at the Chelsea restaurant until she fulfilled her mother's ambition for her by marrying a title so that she could spend the rest of her life swanning around a country estate, decorating the pages of *Country Life*, while a nanny raised her kids...

Not that the problem had been all her fault.

The truth was that he'd never been able to think

straight around Louise and it had been ten times worse since she'd returned from a summer spent in Italy with a full set of curves, blonde curls that looked as if they had been tousled by some dark-eyed Latin and eyes that seemed to mock him.

If she hadn't been his cousin...

But she was. Family. Which meant that after college she'd joined the company, working in *his* restaurant, a situation about as restful as ploughing a minefield; you just never knew when the next explosion was going to happen.

The effect on the staff had been bad enough, but when a particularly disruptive outburst had involved a group of diners he'd had no choice but to fire her on the spot. No choice...

He could cheerfully throttle Jack for putting him in this position.

All the time he'd been in Qu'Arim, setting up the new restaurant, he'd been doing his best to convince himself that his half-brother didn't know what he was talking about.

Obviously he was right about the need to bring in some heavyweight PR muscle. It was a different world from the dreary post-war era; when his grandfather had opened his first restaurant, people had flocked to eat good Italian food served in warm and welcoming surroundings. Under the control of his father and uncle, they'd grown complacent.

They'd been living off reputation, history, for too long. The business had stagnated. The restaurant in Qu'Arim was just the beginning of a new era of global expansion, but to make it work they needed someone who could update the image, get them reviewed, talked about; re-define them not just as a London, but a worldwide 'A-list' restaurant group.

Except that it wasn't 'they' any more.

The future of the company was in his hands and his alone. *He* needed someone. And his brother had made it clear that he didn't just need someone with Louise's talent to take up the challenge.

He needed Louise.

Of course, Jack, having dropped that little bombshell, had waltzed off back to New York leaving him to convince Louise to drop everything and come and work for him.

Yes, well. Having driven her away in the first place, he had to be the one to convince her to return. Whatever it took. Because it seemed to him that just at this moment Louise needed him, just a little, too, whether she'd admit it or not.

He wasn't fooling himself that it would be easy. Louise might have been a useless *maître d'*, more interested in flirting with the customers than doing her job, but since then she'd carved out a brilliant career for herself in marketing and PR. Her client list included one of the most successful restaurant chains in the country. She knew everyone in the business. Everyone in the media. And her mother's high society family gave her an in with the social elite. She *was* 'A' list.

She was also bright enough to know that Bella Lucia needed her a lot more than she needed Bella Lucia.

That he needed her a lot more than she needed him.

If the situation were reversed, if he were in her shoes, he knew he wouldn't listen to one word she had to say until she was on her knees, begging.

He hoped, for his knees' sake, that she wasn't inclined to carry a grudge that far.

Fat chance, he thought, checking the time.

If he shifted himself, he should catch her leaving the office. It wouldn't be so easy for her to ignore him face to face.

'You are a wonder, Louise.' Oliver Nash had waited while she locked up, walked her down to the street and now continued to hold her hand long after it had ceased to be the kind of handshake that concluded a successful meeting. 'Are you going to let me take you to dinner somewhere special? So that I can thank you properly?'

'You'll get my account at the end of the month, Oliver. Prompt payment is all the thanks I need.'

'One of these days you'll make my day and say yes.'

She laughed. 'One of these days I'll say yes, you old fraud, and scare you half to death. Go home to your lovely wife.'

'You know me too well,' he said, then as he bent to kiss her cheek she saw Max leaning against his muscular sports car, watching them.

'Dumped your toy boy for a sugar-daddy, Lou?' he asked.

Louise was thankful that the shadows were deep enough to disguise the flush that had darkened her cheeks. Even now he only had to look at her, speak to her, be in the same room, to send a shiver of something dark, something dangerous, rippling through her body. To disturb the even tenor of her life.

Not that there had been much that was even about it in the last few months.

Oliver, his hand still firmly holding hers, raised a brow a fraction of an inch and, since there was no way to avoid making introductions, she said, 'Oliver, I don't believe you know my…' She caught herself. She was still readjusting to her new identity. Still forgot… 'I don't believe you know Max Valentine. Max, Oliver Nash is a valued client; the chairman of the Nash Group.'

'Fast food?' Max replied.

'Fast profit,' Oliver replied, more amused than annoyed at being the butt of a younger man's jealousy. 'How's business in the slow food sector?'

The exchange, unpleasant though it was, had given her time to recover, put up the barriers with a distant smile, and she stepped in before it deteriorated further.

'I'll see you tomorrow, Oliver,' she said.

'You'll be all right?' He looked up as a thin, icy rain began to fall, then at Max. 'I'd be happy to give you a lift.'

'Louise and I have business to discuss, Nash,' Max intervened, his hand at her elbow, before she could be tempted to let Oliver chauffeur her as far as the nearest underground station in his Rolls. 'Family business.'

His hand was barely touching her. Max never touched her if he could help it, not since that summer before she'd gone away to Italy; after that everything had changed.

They had changed. Become unsettlingly aware of each other in a way that, for cousins, wasn't quite…decent.

Except that now she knew they weren't cousins. That she'd been adopted…

Carefully lifting her arm away, she said, 'Office hours are from ten until six, Max—'

'It's nearly eight.'

He didn't look at his watch and she wondered exactly how long he'd been waiting for her to emerge from her office. Her PA had left a little after six—she had a life—and it must have been before then, or how would he have known she was still on the premises?

She refused to feel guilty about that. Or rise to his bait. She didn't have to explain herself to him. To anybody.

'For valued clients,' she said, 'office hours are infinitely expandable.'

'Infinitely?'

She ignored the innuendo. What she did, whom she did it with, was nothing to do with him.

'If you want to discuss business,' she advised, 'I suggest you call my secretary tomorrow and make an appointment. I may have an hour to spare some time next week.'

She turned to Oliver, said, 'Thanks for the offer, but I won't take you out of your way.' She kissed his cheek. 'I'll see you tomorrow at the photo-shoot.'

Neither she nor Max spoke until the Rolls had pulled away from the kerb. Then she turned to him, said, 'Aren't you missing something, Max?'

'A PR consultant?' he offered.

She shook her head. 'I was referring to your usual accessory blonde. I imagine they have names, but it's so hard to keep up.'

She gained a certain amount of pleasure in seeing him clamp down hard, forced for once to hold his tongue, keep his temper in check. Taking unfair advantage of his predicament, she looked up and down the nearly empty street as if his latest airhead might have wandered off to do some window-shopping.

'Maybe it's a little cold for such delicate creatures to be out,' she added, even as she mentally slapped her wrist for goading him when he couldn't retaliate. But she owed him for that toy boy/sugar-daddy remark. 'No, I've just remembered. At the Christmas party you were flirting with Maddie, but she left with Jack, didn't she? The brother who inherited your father's good manners.'

'According to Jack,' he said, 'the only blonde I need at the moment is you.'

'Really?' She tutted. 'Then you're really going to have to try harder, aren't you?'

And, having done with Max, she raised her hand to summon a cruising taxi. He beat her to the door, opened it, climbed in after her.

'Excuse me but this is my taxi. You have a car,' she reminded him.

'We have to talk.'

'You have to talk. I don't have to listen.'

He didn't wait for an answer but gave the driver her address.

'Hijacking my taxi isn't going to get you what you want,' she said.

'What will?' he asked, sitting back in the far corner of the cab, as far from her as he could get.

That didn't please her either.

'Nothing. I have a thriving business, more clients than I can handle. Why would I be interested in leaving that to work for Bella Lucia? More to the point, why would I spare one minute of my time to listen to you?'

'You're family, Lou. That should be enough.'

'Family? Haven't you been paying attention, Max? That was all just a pretty fiction invented by the Valentines. Your parents, the people who pretended to be my parents. If you're looking for a family connection you've come to the wrong person.'

'Don't be ridiculous. Of course you're family—'

She arched a brow. 'If you've come to demand my loyalty, you're going to have to try a little harder.'

'Not demand—'

She cut him off before he could perjure himself.

'As I recall, being "family"…' she made those irritating little quote marks with her fingers; irritating Max when she had the upper hand was so satisfying '…wasn't enough the last time I was on the payroll. It certainly didn't save me from the humiliation of being sacked in front of an entire restaurant full of diners. I'm sorry, Max, but I don't see the attraction of working for you. I may be blonde, but I'm not dumb.'

'That was a long time ago, Lou.'

'Yes, it was, but what's changed, hmm? You're still treating me like some stupid girl who doesn't know her left from her right. Insulting me in front of an important client. Ignoring my wishes. Well, I've got news for you: I'm not a girl, I'm a fully grown woman and I've built up a successful business from nothing, just the way William Valentine did. You should try it some time, then you might have a little more respect.'

She swallowed. Wished she hadn't said that. Bella Lucia was Max's life. He worked harder than anyone to make it a success. If it had gone down in the recent financial crisis, no one would have been hit harder, or deserved it less.

It was always the same. The minute she was with him, she lost her head, stopped behaving like a rational woman.

She leaned forward, rapped sharply on the driver's window. 'Pull over, please.'

The cabbie pulled into the kerb, but Max didn't move. 'This won't go away, Lou.'

Probably not, but she was tired, she had another long day ahead of her tomorrow, and while a row with Max was always exhilarating she discovered that she wasn't enjoying this one.

'You want me to get down on my knees and beg, is that it?' he pressed.

That was almost too tempting, but Max, on his

knees, would not be a supplicant. He would simply be demonstrating—at least in his own eyes—that he was bigger than she was. That he could forgive and forget. That in clinging to her grudge, she hadn't been able to move on. As he knelt at her feet his eyes would still be telling her that he was the winner.

'All I want,' she said, carefully, slowly, 'is for you to listen to what I'm saying. I'm saying good-night, Max.'

For a moment she thought he was going to protest, force the issue, but then without another word he opened the door and stepped out of the cab, handing the driver a note to cover her fare home—still trying to keep control—and, shrugging his collar up against the rain, he began to walk back to his car.

Louise, left in the cab, was shaking, hating Max for putting her through that, hating herself for caring.

'Is that it?' The driver, having clearly heard everything, turned around. 'Do you want me to drive on? You're not going to change your mind and want me to go after him? Once I turn the corner I'll be locked in the one-way system and there'll be no way back.'

Max could do nothing but walk away. Acknowledge that, having behaved like a moron, he'd got no more than he deserved. What made it worse was that he wasn't like that; at least not with anyone else. He made an exception for Louise.

She never failed to bring out the worst in him.

He only had to look at her and he reverted from civilised man into some kind of Neanderthal.

Maybe she was right, he thought, hunching his shoulders against the icy rain that matched his mood. Nothing had changed. They hadn't been able to work together all those years ago and time had done nothing to mellow either of them.

He'd made the offer but she wasn't interested.

He stopped, blew out a long breath that smoked in the cold air. If someone had made him an offer like that, he wouldn't have been impressed either.

He'd wasted a perfectly good opportunity. He'd planned to ask her to join him for a drink, a meal maybe, and when he'd turned up just after six he'd thought he'd timed it just right. It had begun to unravel from the minute he'd arrived when her assistant, who had already had her coat on, had told him that Lou was in a meeting that was likely to go on for a while, but he could wait if he wanted to.

Sitting around in the outer office waiting for her attention wasn't what he'd had in mind and he should have left then, but, having wound himself up to see her, he'd chosen to wait in his car.

How long could she be?

Too long.

He'd had time to dwell on the memory of the Christmas party. Another failure. He'd known how bruised she must be feeling. Discovering that you were adopted at her age must be like having the solid ground beneath your feet turn to quicksand.

He'd planned to talk to her, let her know that he was there for her, but then she'd turned up in that outrageous outfit with some underage muscle-bound jerk on her arm.

On one level he'd known that it was just her way of showing the older generation, her parents, his father, just how angry she was with all of them for lying to her and he didn't blame her for that.

On a more primitive level…

He shook his head. He should have made more of an effort, he knew. Called her, found time for her, given her a chance to sound off and get it out of her system. He'd been busy, they'd both been busy, but how long did a phone call take?

Not that she'd needed him; the Australian might have been on the young side, but he'd had shoulders wide enough for half a dozen women to weep onto at once.

He'd just got to the stage of telling himself if he'd been there for her she wouldn't have needed to reach for a stranger when she'd walked out of the building with Oliver Nash, at which point he'd offered a classic demonstration of how to make a fool of yourself without really trying.

Only Louise could do that to him.

He flipped open his cell phone, called Louise's number. *This is not personal,* he told himself. *This is not for me, it's for Bella Lucia.* If he could just stop thinking of her as a difficult, disturbing nuisance, start treating her as the talented professional she undoubtedly was, start listening instead of jumping in with both feet…

This time when the voicemail prompted him to leave a message, he said, 'Louise, I know you're busy.' He paused. Whatever it took… 'When you have a moment I'd be grateful if you could spare me an hour to talk about the future, about Bella Lucia—'

'Max…' Lou's voice cut in. He stared at the phone, frowned. Could you override voicemail and take the call?

'Max!'

He spun around.

Louise was caught in the light from the store windows, raindrops glistening in her hair, on the shoulders of her long black coat.

She'd ditched the cab, come after him, and for a moment he couldn't find the breath to speak.

'Louise…I was just leaving a message.'

'I heard you.' She was almost smiling, he thought. 'You were so polite. You must be really desperate.' Then, when he didn't move, she spread her hands and glanced up at the sky, said, 'So? Are we going to stand out here in the rain, or did you have a plan?'

'A drink? Dinner?' he said, scarcely able to believe his luck. She'd come back. 'I know this really good Italian restaurant in the King's Road.'

'Dinner,' she said, 'but somewhere neutral. Not Bella Lucia.'

He clamped his jaw shut, suspecting that she was trying to provoke him. Hoping he'd give her another excuse to turn her back on him.

'Anywhere,' he said. 'You decide.'

The restaurant she chose was close to her office and she was greeted with warmth by the staff. This, rather than Bella Lucia, was clearly the restaurant she used to meet with her clients, with the media people she was wooing.

His failure.

They were shown to their table, served quickly and efficiently, left to themselves and, much as it pained him to admit it, on this occasion she'd made the right choice. If they'd gone to one of his restaurants, his attention would have been constantly distracted by what was happening around them. His ears tuned to the reactions of fellow diners, listening out for problems instead of to her.

He'd seen his father act that way. The business had always been more important to him than anything. Anyone.

He'd tried to emulate him in business, if not in his personal life.

Tonight he needed to focus his full attention on Louise, put his whole heart into getting her on board.

It wasn't difficult. At seventeen, when she'd returned from Italy a newly minted woman, she'd been stunning. The years since had only added layers of character, style, polish and it was easy to see why a man of any age would want to worship at her feet. He couldn't afford to join them.

'How was your trip to Australia?' he asked. 'Melbourne, wasn't it? Did you enjoy it? What's it like?'

'Is that code for would it make a suitable venue for a Bella Lucia restaurant?'

She was warning him to back off, he realised, telling him that her other, newly discovered, family was nothing to do with him. He wanted to dispute that. She was a Valentine and all her family were important. This was not the time, however.

'Are you suggesting that I have a one-track mind?' he asked.

She took a sip of water. Said nothing.

Obviously she was.

'So?' he pressed, turning her question to his own advantage. Getting her to open up about Bella Lucia. 'Melbourne? What do you think?'

'I think you're leaping to the conclusion that I give a damn about Bella Lucia.'

'It's fed, sheltered and kept the designer clothes on your back for two-thirds of your life,' he reminded her. 'Paid for the apartment that Uncle John gave you when you decided it was time to leave home. I think you might give the tiniest damn, don't you?'

It was cruel. She blushed, swallowed, but he'd got her. She might be angry, bitter, but she knew what she owed to John and Ivy Valentine. She might not want to play happy families at the moment, but she wasn't a fool, she must know she couldn't walk away from them that easily and if she needed reminding, he'd be happy to oblige.

But while he'd hooked her, she wasn't happy about it.

'How do you plan a marketing campaign?' he asked, bowing to her expertise, using flattery to reel her in. 'Where do you start?'

For a moment she resisted, toyed with the linguine she'd ordered. He didn't leap in, try to push her.

'The first thing is to establish the brand,' she said, at last.

'Brand?' He frowned. 'We're not one of Nash's fast-food outlets.'

She dismissed his remark with an impatient gesture. 'Don't be so narrow in your thinking, Max.' Then, 'What do you think brings someone through the door of a Bella Lucia restaurant?'

'It depends which someone. Which restaurant. They're each unique. Individual in style, atmosphere. A man who met his colleagues for a business lunch at Berkeley Square would probably choose to take his wife for dinner in Knightsbridge, might have a coming-of-age celebration for one of his children in Chelsea.'

'Who would he take to Qu'Arim?'

He thought about it. Thought who he'd take there, then shook his head to clear the image he had of Louise there. With him.

'A woman he was in love with,' he said. Then, 'The oasis is the very essence of romance.'

'A very over-used word.' She regarded him for a moment, then said, 'If it was a fabric, what would it be?'

'A fabric?'

'Cotton?' she offered. 'No? Cashmere? Tweed? Velvet? Linen? Silk?' She ticked them off on her fingers.

'Silk,' he said. 'With a touch of cashmere.'

'And if it was a time of day?'

'Night,' he said, before she could list the options. 'Black with a sliver of moon, stars close enough to touch.'

'Every man a desert sheikh, every woman his captive slave? That's not romance, Max, that's a sexual fantasy.'

'Is that bad?'

'Probably not,' she admitted, a touch ruefully. 'It's not very PC to say this but sex sells.' Then, more to herself than him, 'I wonder what a woman's response would be.'

His smile was slow, thoughtful. 'I'll take you there. Then you can tell me.'

'I'm the one conducting a market survey,' she said, swiftly evading the elephant trap she'd so carelessly dug for herself. 'Tell me more.'

He needed no prompting to describe the setting of the resort, the undiluted luxury. 'We're very fortunate, Lou. Surim could have had his pick of international restaurateurs.'

'The old school tie is still worth something, then.'

'If you're going to save someone from a beating, it might as well be a future head of state,' he agreed.

Louise shook her head. 'Sorry. I didn't mean to be quite that cynical. I know you're good friends. Do you still play polo in his team?'

'Not recently. It's tough finding time to keep match fit.'

'You need to get out from behind the desk, Max. All work and no play—'

'Says the lady who's just worked a ten-hour day.'

'Twelve, actually.' She pulled a face, shrugged. 'I was at the office at eight. But it's only while I'm working on the HOTfood relaunch.' Then, quickly, moving on before he could say anything about pots and kettles, 'Okay, tell me about the food at the new restaurant. Mediterranean? Arabic? What is there beyond tabbouleh, hummus, the mezza?'

He smiled at her ignorance. 'Arab cuisine was once the most sophisticated in the entire world, Louise, embraced by the mediaeval courts of Europe.'

'Really? I like that. Tell me more.'

As she pushed him for details, forcing him to reach beyond the basics, Max actually began to relax, feel that this was, after all, going to be possible.

'I meant it when I said I'd take you there. I'd like you to see it for yourself.'

'And after Qu'Arim, what then?' she asked, not picking up on his invitation, but not refusing it, either. 'How far and how fast are you planning to take this?'

'How big is the world? The Americas, Asia, Europe.'

'Europe? Have you considered Meridia?'

'Obviously it's on the list.'

'I suggest you put it at the top. Bella Lucia catered for the coronation, and now that your sister is Queen I'd have a bidding war from the gossip mags to cover the opening of a new restaurant there.'

'We don't display our clientele for the media, Lou. We give them privacy.'

'Okay, I could use that as an angle. Pictures of the interior pre-opening offering a glimpse of something most people will never see. Mystery, privacy, the unattainable. A glimpse of lace is always more intriguing than total nudity.'

Max found himself staring at the cashmere sweater Louise was wearing. It was some complicated wrap-around thing that crossed over her breasts, offering no more than a suggestion of cleavage, a promise of hidden delights. She didn't have to explain the allure of the unattainable to him. He'd lived with it for as long as he could remember.

CHAPTER TWO

'THAT rather depends on who's wearing the lace,' Max said abruptly. 'And what she looks like when she's shed it.'

Louise raised an eyebrow. What was eating *him*?

'You've spent more time in Meridia than I have,' he went on, before she could ask. 'What are the options for us there?'

She shrugged, let it go. 'What are the limits of your imagination? Somewhere really sumptuous high up in the old part of the capital, near the castle. Or maybe something completely different. A place where families could sit outside and eat in the summer. Maybe somewhere with a dock, since everybody seems to have a boat.'

Seeing it in her mind's eye, she was suddenly seized with enthusiasm, her thoughts running faster than she could say them.

'A lakeside pavilion, perhaps. Something…'

'Something what?' Max prompted.

'Um… Something simple, uncluttered, informal,'

she said, suddenly realising that she was using her hands to describe her thoughts. She'd always done that. Her mother used to say it was her Italian ancestry coming out. Nonsense, of course. There was no Italian connection; John Valentine had been born before his father had ever met Lucia. But then her entire history had been founded on lies…

'How soon can you wind up your business and join us, Louise?' he asked, cutting into the black thoughts that threatened to engulf her.

Bringing her back to earth.

'Excuse me?' Her tone was deceptively mild. Her assistant would have winced. But for a few minutes there she'd let herself imagine a different future, forget reality, but Max never let her down. Already he was assuming he'd won, but then he was a man programmed never to lose.

'Why on earth would I give up a business I've built from scratch to come and work for you?'

Max smiled. 'It's a bit late to start pretending you're not interested, Lou.'

'I…' In her enthusiasm she'd leaned into the table and suddenly realised just how close they were. Close enough for her to drown in dangerously deep blue eyes that had been mesmerising her for as long as she could remember. Close enough to catch the warm, male scent of his skin. To feel the tug of something she'd been resisting since she was old enough to understand that it was wrong.

She sat back, putting enough distance between them to feel, if not safe, then in control. 'My interest is purely professional, Max.'

There had been a time she would have died of happiness to have Max wanting her, needing her, but there was no way she'd give up her independence and crawl back under the shelter of the Valentine umbrella. Not now. She didn't need them. Didn't need him.

'Apart from anything else, I'm considering branching out myself,' she said, 'opening an office in Melbourne, using that as my base in Australia.'

He looked as if she'd hit him with a club.

She might have enjoyed that more if she hadn't been swept away, just for a moment, thinking what might have been. If anyone but Max were involved.

'You have a life, a family here,' he protested.

'You think so? Now Dad's skeletons have climbed out of the closet I find myself excess to requirements.'

Max looked as if he was going to deny it, but they'd both seen just how far John Valentine would go for sons he'd only just discovered existed. Even when one of them had nearly ruined the company, he'd still been sheltered, cared for. Loved.

'Have you told your parents? That you're considering moving to Australia?'

Louise swallowed. 'Not yet.'

'You're hurting, I understand that, but don't cut yourself off from your family, Louise.'

Family, family... He was always going on about the precious family; as a boy he'd spent more time with hers than with his own...

'I take it the toy boy is part of the plan,' he said, an edge to his voice that could have cut glass.

Relieved to be out of the quicksand of family relationships, she managed an arch, 'Are you, by any chance, referring to Cal Jameson?'

'If he's the one who was all over you at the Christmas party, then yes, that's who I mean.'

'He wasn't all over me,' she declared.

So much for her vow to keep her cool. With Max, that was only ever going to be a temporary measure.

'Oh, please. You arrived at the Christmas party dressed like some centrefold Santa—'

'I always come as Santa!'

With the long-running friction between her father and Uncle Robert—Max's father—the family Christmas party was a minefield of tension at the best of times and she'd taken to turning up in a Santa suit bearing a sack filled with clever little presents matched to each member of the family. Her contribution to peace on earth in the Valentine family; bath oil on troubled waters.

This year, though, there had been two new family members; the sons that John Valentine hadn't known existed until a few months ago. Her only reason for pouring oil would have been to set fire to it so she'd abandoned the traditional 'ho, ho, ho' Santa outfit in favour of a red suede miniskirt with matching boots, a white angora crop top and a mistletoe navel ring—one that lit up and flashed in the dark.

Her cheeks heated at the memory. With the twenty-twenty vision of hindsight it was obvious that inviting Cal to kiss her under the mistletoe—purely to wind up a scowling Max—had been a mistake.

She should have anticipated that he'd ask, 'How far under…'

'I have family in Australia,' she said, quickly, before Max made the kind of remark guaranteed to provoke her beyond reason. 'A married sister.'

'You barely know her,' he pointed out, infuriatingly reasonable.

'And already I like her a lot better than I like you. Nothing has changed, Max!' She stood up, desperate to escape, desperate for air. 'I don't need this.'

He was on his feet, blocking her exit before she could take a step. 'You need it,' he said. 'You need it like breathing. Admit it. You're lit up with excitement at the thought of coming back.' She shook her head, but he repeated the words. 'Lit up like the Christmas tree in Trafalgar Square.'

'No!'

'You're a Valentine, Lou. Bella Lucia is in your blood.'

She almost gasped at his lack of understanding. Where had he been the last few months? Had he any idea…?

No. Of course not. Max didn't do 'feeling'. He was so utterly focussed on Bella Lucia, so absorbed by it, that he didn't need normal human emotion.

Well, she would just have to explain it to him. In words of one syllable…

'Is that what you really think?' she demanded.

'It's what I know. It's what I see—'

'Shall I tell you what I'll be doing tomorrow?' she demanded, not interested in what he could see. The question was purely rhetorical; she was going to tell him whether he wanted to know or not. 'I'm going to be taking afternoon tea in the restaurant on the top floor of the National Portrait Gallery. Minimalist elegance, smoked salmon sandwiches and great views should conversation prove difficult.'

'Why should it prove difficult?' Then, barely able to conceal his satisfaction, 'You're kissing off the Australian?'

'What? No…' She swiped at the air in front of her face, pushing his interruption away, pushing him away, the pervasive power of his presence. 'Cal isn't…'

'What?'

'Cal isn't any of your business,' she snapped. 'I'm meeting my mother, tomorrow.' Then, just to be sure he understood, 'Not your aunt, Max. Not Ivy Valentine.' Not the woman who, all her life, she'd been told was her mother. 'I'm meeting Patricia Simpson Harcourt, the total stranger who, it seems, actually gave birth to me. The woman who'll be able to tell me who my father was, what he looked like, because the only thing I do know about him is that he wasn't John Valentine.'

'Louise—'

'You do see, don't you?' she asked, cutting short his attempt to interrupt, to tell her that it didn't matter. Because it did. 'You do see how wrong you are? Valentine blood does not flow through my veins. Not one drop of it. The only liquid connecting me to the Valentine family is the ink on the adoption certificate.'

'Please, Lou.' He caught her hand, refusing to let her pass him. Escape. 'Don't do anything hasty. Bella Lucia needs you.' Then, almost as if it hurt him to say the words, he finally said what she'd always wanted to hear. 'I need you.'

His words brought her up short. She might mock his dedication, but Max had always been the one everyone else depended on. The one that everyone else turned to in a crisis. For him to admit that he needed anyone had to be a first. For him to admit that he needed her…

'Y-you sacked me,' she said, more to remind herself what he'd done than jog his memory. It had been a scene neither of them was likely to forget. 'In front of the entire restaurant. You didn't care that I was family then—'

'That was the problem, Lou,' he cut in. Then, more gently, 'That was always the problem.'

'I-I don't understand.'

'Don't you?'

Of course she did. As a girl she'd worshipped him. She should have grown up, got over it. It hadn't worked out like that. Quite the contrary. Even now he had the power to reduce her to a gibbering idiot, a mass of exposed hormones. All it took was the touch of his hand to turn her to jelly. If she didn't get out of here now…

'Don't you?' he insisted. 'Are you really that stupid?'

'Thanks for that, Max,' she said, snatching away her hand. For a moment she'd thought that maybe, just maybe, they could make a fresh start but she'd been fooling herself. 'You've just reminded me why I'd rather starve than work for you.'

As Louise strode towards the door a waiter held out her coat. She didn't pause to let him help her into it, but grabbed it and as he leapt to open the door walked out into the cold rain.

She glanced up and down the street, hoping to spot

a cruising cab, but there wasn't a sign of one and, without stopping to put on her coat, she began to walk.

'Not one drop…'

Max was rooted to the spot for long seconds as her words echoed in his head, as the reality of what that meant sank in.

'Shall I bring the bill, sir?'

The waiter's voice jerked him out of the moment of revelation and he realised that he was letting Louise walk away, that if he didn't do something to stop her right now he'd have lost her, or, worse, that she wouldn't stop walking until she was out of all their lives. Not just lost to him, but to the family who loved her.

Not bothering to reply, he tossed a credit card on the table and headed for the door.

The same waiter, apparently anticipating his reaction, was holding his coat out and the door open so that nothing should impede him.

Louise was walking swiftly along the street, the high heels of her boots ringing against the wet pavement, her coat trailing from her hand. The fact that she was oblivious to the rain now coming down in torrents, soaking her hair, soaking her through to the skin, gave him hope.

She was upset, angry. If she didn't care, she would be neither.

'Louise!' His voice echoed along the empty street, but she neither slowed nor quickened her pace, made no sign that she'd heard him. 'Wait!'

A cab turned the corner and, ignoring him, she raised a hand to hail it, forcing him to sprint along the pavement to head her off.

'Here's a point for you,' he said breathlessly as he leaned against the door, blocking her escape.

She didn't protest, just turned away as another cab appeared, but he reached out, caught her hand before she could summon it.

'Here's a point for you,' he repeated more gently as with his free hand he picked a strand of wet hair from her cheek and tucked it behind her ear. Held it there. 'You were adopted.'

'Hallelujah,' she said, but she didn't move, didn't toss her head to dislodge his hand. 'For once in your life you were listening.'

Her words were spiky but her voice was ragged, hurting.

She was looking up at him, her eyes leaden in the street lighting, her lashes clumped together by the rain pouring down her cheeks. Or maybe it was tears and for a moment the impulse to kiss her almost overwhelmed him.

Not now...

He'd paid heed to the warning voice in his head all his adult life. Kept his distance even when the only thing in his head had been to stop her anger with his mouth, knowing that she wanted it, too; was goading him, tormenting him, tempting him to do something about the primal response that arc'd between them whenever they were in the same room; urging him to self-destruct. Now there was no impediment, no barrier, only hard-won self-restraint, some instinct warning him that this was not the moment.

'I was listening,' he told her, his voice cool, even though every other part of him was burning hot.

'So?'

So kissing her suddenly seemed the most important thing in the entire world.

This is about the restaurant, not you!

He ignored the voice of common sense. This was important…

'So you're not my cousin, Louise.'

'Give the man a coconut—'

Her skin felt like wet silk beneath his fingers. Her mouth was full and dark and suddenly all the wasted 'touch not' years crowded in on him, urging him to taste it, taste her.

'And if we're not cousins,' he continued, a little shakily, 'we don't have a problem, do we?'

Not now, idiot! Bella Lucia is more important than scratching a ten year itch.

But…

You'll blow the whole deal if you kiss her, because it wouldn't stop at a kiss. She'd come along for the ride, she wouldn't be able to help herself, but what then? She'd never forgive you...

But she'd come...

'We don't?' she asked, a tiny frown creasing the centre of her forehead. She drew in a breath as if to pursue it further, then shook her head, clearly thinking better of it. 'You're taking me for granted, Max,' she said.

'No...'

He denied it, but without sufficient conviction to stop her.

'Yes! You believe that all you have to do is turn up, snap your fingers and I'll fall in line. I have a career, a successful business, a life of my own—'

'I know,' he said. 'I know. You owe me nothing. But think of Bella Lucia. Think of your father...'

She jerked free of his touch then and he knew that in clumsily mentioning her father, he'd made things worse rather than better. She could have no idea how he'd felt as he'd watched her with her parents. Proper parents who always put her first. Doted on her...

She was hurting too much to listen to him tell her how lucky she was. How lucky she'd been all her life. Right now, he suspected, there was nothing he could say that would help. Maybe he would, after all, have been better served by less thought, more action but he'd missed the moment, allowed her to climb back on her high horse.

'Enough,' he said, letting it go. 'You're wet through.' He took her coat, wrapped it around her shoulders. 'You need to go home, get warm.' He opened the cab door, saw her safely in and this time resisted the temptation to join her, but instead, on an impulse, said, 'Would you like some company tomorrow?'

'Tomorrow?'

Louise couldn't think straight. They weren't cousins. Well, she'd understood that. In theory. She just hadn't thought through what that meant. Hadn't anticipated exactly how she'd feel in that dangerous moment when, for a heartbeat, she'd been sure Max had been about to kiss her. Finally. At last...

'When you meet this woman who says she's your mother,' he prompted, bringing her back to earth.

'She *is* my mother.'

'Is she? Really? More so than Ivy? I'm sorry, but it's hard for me to get my head around that.'

'Really?' She heard the sarcasm fuelled by frustration, disappointment, dripping from her voice. Why hadn't he kissed her? What else could he have meant when he'd said they 'didn't have a problem'? 'Well, if you find it hard, why don't you try putting yourself in my shoes?'

'Don't be so defensive, Lou.'

'Defensive?' He thought she was being defensive? 'You think I should be sweet, biddable, good little Louise and not make a fuss, hmm?'

'Sweet? Biddable?' He shook his head, might have been fighting a smile; his face was shadowed and it was hard to tell. 'Sorry, sweetheart, I know that you've managed to fool the older generation with that myth since you were old enough to work out that a smile would bring you more than a scowl, but you've always managed to keep that side of yourself well hidden around me,' he said. Seeing her sarcasm and raising it to scorn.

About to respond in kind, tell him that if she did, it was his fault, she clamped her mouth shut. The truth was that he brought out the very worst in her, that even now, angry as she was, all she wanted was to drag him into the cab with her and be very, very bad indeed.

She took a slow breath. She was losing control. Again. She'd got away with it once this evening; she wasn't going to risk it twice.

She'd always known she would do what he wanted, that despite everything she owed the family who'd raised her that kind of loyalty, but she hated the fact that it was Max who was doing the arm-twisting. She'd do it, but on her own terms.

Set her own price.

Not money…

And an idea slipped into her mind and lodged there.

She shook her head, forced herself to look at him. 'I don't need anyone to hold my hand, Max.'

'You have no idea how you'll feel. I won't intrude, but if you knew that there was a friend nearby. Someone you could talk to…'

'You?' she enquired, coolly, rescuing him as he ran out of platitudes. 'Can you really spare the time? With all those restaurants to run,' she reminded him.

'I'll make time.'

Her only response was to raise one eyebrow. It was not original, but he got the point.

'I promise.'

'Oh, right. So tell me, Max, would that be like the time you promised to escort me to my school prom?' She didn't wait for Max to come up with some plausible excuse for leaving her all dressed up, without a date, for the biggest night of her young life. Her father wouldn't let her out that late with anyone else. Not that she'd wanted anyone else. 'At the very moment when all the phones in the world apparently stopped working,' she added.

'You know what happened,' he protested. 'Dad was short-handed in the restaurant.' And he was the one thrown back on the defensive, dragging fingers through his thick, cropped hair in a gesture that was achingly familiar. 'Before I knew it, it was gone ten and there was no way I could get there in time. You know what it's like—'

'Yes, Max, I know.' She knew only too well what his promises were worth. 'It was like the time you promised to pick me up and take me to the airport.'

He frowned.

'No? Well, you didn't remember then, either, but don't worry, it's not one of those once-in-a-lifetime, never-to-be-repeated experiences; there's always another plane.' She suspected she was hurting herself more than him by dredging up all the times when, caught up in work, he'd let her down. But for once he was forced to listen and she persisted. 'And as for the time you left me stranded—'

'I'll be there, Louise,' he said, cutting her off. 'I'll be there,' he repeated, but gently.

Gently, she thought, he might just destroy her. She couldn't allow him to be gentle.

'If nothing more important comes up.'

But she was safe. Something always did. She knew that once he was working Max forgot everything, everyone else. That he always put the success of the restaurants, his responsibility towards the staff, before his personal life. Maybe that was the reason for the constant stream of girlfriends. It didn't, as she could testify, do much for a girl's self-esteem to be stood up for a restaurant.

'I won't hold my breath.'

Not waiting for more protestations of sincerity, she reached forward and pulled the door shut, gave the driver her address and huddled down beneath her coat, her teeth chattering as reaction set in.

Max watched as the taxi pulled away, disappeared into the murk of a wet January night, hard pressed to decide whether he was angrier with Louise for being so unreasonable, so prickly, or himself for not doing better. Not that there was anything he could do about it now.

What he could do, must do, was return to the restaurant and make his excuses for their abrupt departure. And give his card to the waiter who'd impressed him with his quick thinking, tell him to call if he ever needed a job.

Even as he did it, he knew that if she could see him Louise would curl her lip, give him the look that said, 'See? Business first, last and always…'

Maybe she had a point, but tomorrow she was guaranteed his undivided attention. Even if the roof fell in at all three London restaurants at the same time he would be there for her and not only because he would do anything to get her on board.

He'd be there because she was in grave danger of cutting all family ties, walking away. Her anger, her sense of betrayal, was clouding her judgement. But then she'd never been without two loving parents. Never, in her whole life, known what it was like to feel alone. Never would, if he had anything to do with it.

At least with him she'd never been afraid to show her feelings. Quite the opposite. And he smiled. For once, that might be a good thing.

Taking his own advice, he thawed out under a hot shower, running through the ideas Louise had tossed out over dinner. He'd just seen expansion as more of the same, but she'd seen the danger of turning Bella Lucia into an upmarket chain, with the expectation that each one would offer the same menu, the same experience, no matter where in the world you happened to be.

That wasn't what they did. Each of their London restaurants was different in atmosphere, style, clientele. They had to carry that across the globe. Use that individuality as their 'brand'.

Already questions were piling up, ideas he wanted to bounce off her; he wanted to be able to pick up the phone now and carry on where they'd left off before he'd blown it all with one careless phrase. What was it she'd said? That she'd rather starve than work for him?

Despite the frustration, he grinned.

Starve? He didn't think so. Bella Lucia had been part of her life since she was old enough to lift a spoon; she'd have come back like a shot if Jack had stayed to run the company.

She didn't have a problem with the business. She had a problem with him.

So what would it take to get her to swallow that bitter pill? What would tempt her to work for him? Keep her from leaving the country and starting up again on the other side of the world?

There had to be a way. There was always a way. For anyone else it would simply be a question of money; how much would it take? But this was more than a job for Louise, just as it was more than a job for him.

For him it had become his life.

What could he offer her that she wouldn't be able to turn down?

And the same internal voice that had warned him so violently against kissing her was now taunting him, saying, *If you'd kissed her she'd be all yours…*

What did you wear to meet your birth mother for the first time? Something sweet and girly? The kind of clothes that a mother would want to see her daughter wearing? The kind of clothes that Ivy had bought for her. Pretty clothes. Good girl clothes. Hair bands, pie-crust frill blouses, modest skirts, an embarrassingly modest sugar-pink prom dress that had made her look exactly her age, rather than all grown up. A dress she'd modified so that the minute she reached the safety of the hotel she was going to replace the ghastly sweetheart bodice with a black strapless top that would knock Max for six.

She'd never been quite the Little-Miss-Perfect

that her mother had believed her to be. Even at sixteen, she'd wanted Max to look at her, to hold her, to desire her. Her deepest longings, darkest thoughts, had always involved him.

How bad was that?

She'd been exhausted when she'd finally fallen into bed, but her sleep had been disturbed by a continuous flow of ideas for Bella Lucia. She should be totally focussed on the final run-up to the HOTfood launch at the end of week, but her sleeping mind had moved on; it was only when she'd tried to interest Max—always too busy to listen—that she'd been jerked awake, shivering.

She had to forget him, forget Bella Lucia, she told herself as she flipped through the classics that were the mainstay of her wardrobe these days. Elegant dresses for the evening, designer suits.

She'd temporarily abandoned them when she was in Australia; staying with Jodie she'd gone beach-girl casual, not just in her clothes, but in her attitude to life. Well, that hadn't lasted long before she'd been summoned home when her father had found a great big hole in the tax fund account. Already it seemed like a lifetime away.

Then her hand brushed against her shock-the-family red suede miniskirt.

It had worked, too.

Her mother had definitely not approved but she

hadn't said a word. Just tightened her lips and forced a smile. Even welcomed Cal to the family party.

Max, of course, as always, had curled his lip and kept his distance.

She could never decide whether that was better or worse than his insults. On this occasion he'd quickly turned to flirting with Maddie, ignoring both her and her outrageous Christmas outfit.

From the way he'd reacted last night, however, it was obvious that he'd taken in every detail. And despite everything she smiled as her fingers lingered against the softness of the leather; no question, he'd noticed.

'Pitiful,' she muttered, pushing the skirt away, trying to push away the memory. Disgusted with herself for behaving so badly.

Certain that Max's perfect recall would be missing when it came to his promise to turn up this afternoon.

He'd have a million more important things to do than hang around an art gallery in the unlikely event that she might need one of his broad shoulders to cry on.

As if.

Not that she cared. It mattered not one jot to her whether he turned up or not. Any more than it mattered which suit, which shoes, she wore today.

She didn't need anyone. Not the mother who'd given her away, not the mother who'd lied to her and definitely not the man whose promises were about as reliable as the forecast of sun on a public holiday.

She blinked back the tears and, catching sight of herself in the mirror, pulled a face.

Oh, for goodness' sake! Who did she think she was kidding? Today of all days she had to look fabulous and twenty minutes later she was on her way to the office wearing a head-turning dark plum suit with a nipped-in waist, a silk camisole a shade or two lighter and ultra high-heeled suede peep-toe shoes that had cost a mint, but exactly matched her suit.

The luscious matching silk underwear she wore purely for her own pleasure.

'You're cutting it fine, Lou.' Gemma, her PA, held out her coat, pointedly. 'There's a taxi waiting for you.'

'Thanks. If Oliver calls back about—'

'I'll handle it. Go.'

'But you'll need…'

'Go!'

'Okay! I'm gone…'

She'd thought the day would drag, but in truth it had flown by with barely a moment in which to draw breath. Cramming in a last-minute meeting had left her with no time to clock-watch, ponder the coming meeting, how it would be to come face to face with the woman who'd given birth to her before surrendering her to a stranger. Suddenly that didn't seem such a great thing. Excitement, anticipation churned with fear in her stomach and she wanted time to slow down. Wanted to put this off...

Wanted someone to hold her hand.

Would he be there? Max...

The clock on the tower of St Martin's-in-the-Fields had already nudged past four as she paid off the taxi and walked through the door of the National Portrait Gallery.

She didn't linger, didn't look around to see if Max had, for once, kept his word. She wanted it too much. Better not to know, to be able to pretend he was there in the shadows watching over her. And if, by some miracle he was there, she wouldn't want him to know how much it mattered. How scared she was. So, looking neither to left nor right, she headed straight for the lift, punched the button for the top floor where the restaurant provided a rooftop view of Trafalgar Square, distant Westminster, the Eye...

She'd heard all about her mother from Jodie, of course, although she suspected that her half-sister had glossed over the bad bits—and there were always difficulties in the mother/ daughter relationship—wanting her to be able to make up her own mind. Knew what to expect. In theory.

She'd seen photographs.

She'd always thought she looked like Ivy Valentine; everyone, even the few members of the family who'd known the truth, had always said how much like Ivy she was—perpetuating the lie.

Once she'd seen a photograph of Patricia Simpson, however, she'd seen the lie for what it was. Here, in the shape of the eyes, the way her hair curved across her forehead, something about the chin, was a genetic imprint that unmistakably linked them and she'd never doubted for a moment that she was looking at her birth mother.

She stepped from the lift, hesitated. Took a moment to steady her breathing, slow her heart-rate, just as she did before a big presentation. Putting on a show…

Then she walked into the restaurant.

She'd imagined looking around, hunting her mother out, but there was no missing her. She might be in her early fifties, but she was still a head-turner.

Her red hair, no doubt kept that way with chemical assistance these days, slid sensuously across her cheek. Her long, finely muscled dancer's legs were crossed to advantage, showing off high insteps, exquisite shoes.

She was sitting by the window, but she wasn't looking at the view. Instead she was chatting to a man sitting at a nearby table, chin propped on her hand, her throaty laugh reaching across the room. He couldn't take his eyes off her and neither could Louise.

Seeing the reality was like the difference between an old black and white movie and Technicolor.

For a moment she couldn't breathe. Couldn't move.

A waiter hovered to seat her, but she ignored him. The rest of the room disappeared. There was only her mother and, as if somehow sensing her presence, Patricia Simpson Harcourt looked up and their eyes connected.

CHAPTER THREE

LOUISE had tried to imagine this moment. Picture it in her mind. What would she say? Would they shake hands? Hug?

Her mother stood up in what appeared to be slow motion and Louise began to walk towards her, barely conscious of a floor that felt like marsh-mallow beneath her feet.

Neither of them said a word, they just reached for each other, clung to each other for what seemed like an age, until gradually the sounds of the restaurant, other people talking, the clink of a spoon, began to impinge on the small bubble of silence and they parted, Patricia holding her at arm's length.

'Well, look at you!' she finally said. 'You're so beautiful.' Then, with a grin, 'And you have such great taste in shoes!'

Louise shook her head. Shoes? 'It's obvious where I got it from...' she began, hesitated, her tongue tripping over the word she'd been rehearsing, but there was no way she could call this glamorous woman "Mother", or "Mum". 'I don't know what to call you,' she said.

There was only the briefest hesitation before she replied, 'Patsy, darling. Call me Patsy.' She turned away quickly, smiled and nodded at a hovering waiter. 'I've already ordered,' she said, sitting down. Then, head slightly to one side, 'Louise? It suits you. I was going to call you…'

'What?'

'Nothing. Pure indulgence.' Then, 'Zoë. I was going to call you Zoë.'

'I'd have liked that.'

'Yes, well, it wasn't meant to be.'

Louise waited. She wanted to ask the big question. *Why?* Instead she said, 'I only found out that I was adopted a few months ago. If I'd known, I'd have looked for you before.'

'Things happen for a reason. Ten years ago I was not the person I am now; I might have been bad for you.' She smiled. 'The earth turns, things change. Now is the right time for us to get to know one another.'

'Maybe…' But it wasn't her mother she was thinking about. What had happened had been out of her control. With Max things were different. It was her decision.

Everything would be so different this time…

Without warning her body seemed to tingle with anticipation, excitement.

'Louise?'

She gave a little shiver. 'Sorry?'

'I said that there's no point in dwelling on what might have been.' Then, looking at her more closely, 'Are you all right? This must all have come as something of a shock to you.'

'No. I'm fine.' …*we don't have a problem…* 'Can I ask you about my father?'

'Oh, well… There's not a lot to tell.'

'His name?' she prompted.

'Jimmy. Jimmy Masters.' She gave a little sigh. 'He rode a motorbike, wore a leather jacket, smouldered like a cut-price James Dean. He was totally irresistible. Not that I tried very hard,' she confessed, with a rueful smile. 'To resist him. He took off, never to be seen again, the minute I told him he was going to be a daddy.' She shook her head. 'I didn't want to give you up, Louise. It was hard, I had no idea how hard it would be, but everyone said you'd have a better life with a good family.' She leaned forward and took her hand. 'I've only got to look at you to know that I made the right decision.'

She did? That wasn't quite what Louise had wanted to hear. She wanted regret, remorse. Instead, beneath that bright, confident smile, Louise realised, Patsy needed to be reassured, to be told that she'd done the right thing.

Just like everyone else, her birth mother wanted her to understand, absolve her from her guilt...

'I've had a lovely life,' Louise said.

It was true, she had.

She'd been cherished, loved, given everything she'd ever wanted. Everything except the truth. The companionship of a sister she hadn't known existed...

They'd all known. Her grandparents, Max's parents. And they'd all lied. The bitterness was as strong, as tangible as the aloes her nanny had painted on her fingernails to stop her from biting them.

But she couldn't get past the fact that she'd had a blessed life. That she owed them for that. She'd always intended to help with Bella Lucia—once Max could bring himself to ask nicely. She would repay them with her time, her skill and then she would be free to do whatever she wanted. Be whoever she wanted to be. The only thing she wasn't prepared to do was give up the business she'd worked so hard to build, give up her independence.

It more important than ever now.

Her rock.

And, in a heartbeat, she understood a little of

what Bella Lucia meant to Max. It had been the one fixed point in his life. When his parents had packed him off to boarding school to get him out of their hair, when Aunt Georgina had disappeared for months on end on some painting expedition with her latest lover, when his father had been drooling over his latest wife, Bella Lucia had been his rock…

While she had two mothers who cared about her, who had ever been there for him? They'd been so close once… Because of what her family had done, their lies, he'd lost that, too.

Without warning tears stung against her lids, not for herself this time, but for Max and to distract her she picked up her bag, opened it, said, 'I've brought you some photographs. If you'd like them?'

And suddenly they were both blinking and laughing as she produced a little wallet filled with her firsts: first steps, first birthday, first day at school in a blazer a size too big with her hat set just so, so that the badge showed…

'Oh, please, put them away and look at them later, or we'll both end up with panda-eyes,' Louise said, torn between laughter and tears. 'I want to hear about you, Patsy. Jodie told me you've just got married again. Tell me about Derek.'

She lit up. 'Every woman should have a man like Derek Harcourt in her life.' As she poured the tea the blaze of diamonds on her left hand caught the lights. 'He really cares about me. Keeps me on the straight and narrow with my diet—I'm a diabetic, did you know?' she said, pulling a face.

'Jodie told me.'

'You'll need to keep an eye on your own health. It's hereditary.'

'I'll take care.' Then, 'Tell me about your honeymoon trip. You went on a cruise?'

'It was heaven…' Once she was off, the conversation never lagged.

They talked about Jodie, Australia, Louise's business. About everything but the Valentine family. It was like talking to someone she'd known all her life. But eventually the conversation came back around to her.

'I have my Derek and Jodie has her Heath. What about you, sweetie?' Patsy asked. 'They say everything happens in threes. Is there anyone special in your life?'

In that split second before she spoke, Louise remembered the way that Max had looked at her. The way she'd felt…

'No,' she said, quickly, but even as the word left her mouth a little voice was saying, *No problem. No impediment. Nothing to stop you…*

Her mother raised one perfectly groomed brow and Louise distracted her with tales about old boyfriends. The ones she might have married if they'd asked.

'Just as well they didn't ask,' she said, laughing. 'It would have been a total disaster.'

She didn't tell her about the one she'd convinced herself was everything she was looking for in a husband: the one who'd told her to stop fooling herself before he'd walked away.

'I hate to say goodbye,' Patsy said as, finally, they walked towards the lift. Then, when she didn't immediately respond, 'You *do* want to see me again?'

Louise, momentarily distracted by the back view of Max, apparently absorbed in a painting, said, 'Yes, yes, of course I do.'

He'd come.

He'd actually turned up, had waited in case she needed him.

'I, um, want to meet Derek, too.'

The lift arrived and Patsy stepped in, holding the door. Louise forced herself not to glance back and stepped in beside her, arranged dinner for the next week, then hugged her mother goodbye on the pavement before seeing her into a taxi.

'You're sure I can't give you a lift?' she asked, from the back of the cab.

'No. I'm fine. I'll give you a call about next week.'

She waited, waved as she drove off. Then turned and walked back into the gallery, took the lift back up to the top floor.

When the doors opened, she saw that Max had not moved and she didn't know whether she was irritated by his certainty that she'd come back, or warmed by the fact that he'd waited for her. There were no clear cut lines with him.

'I thought it was best to stay put,' he said, as she held the door and he stopped pretending, joined her in the lift, 'or we might have been chasing one another around the houses for the next ten minutes.'

'Only if I came back,' she pointed out, trying not to smile, but without much success.

'True.' He seemed to be finding it easy enough to keep a straight face. Then, 'You're very like her.'

'Yes. It's strange. All my life people have been telling me I'm like my… Like Ivy Valentine…'

'She's still your mother, Lou. She was the one who raised you. And you are like her. Okay, some of it's superficial, chance. Your colouring, height. But it's not just that. You hold your head the way she does, you use the same gestures. You have her class.'

'You don't think Patsy has class?'

'Patsy?'

'It's a bit late in the day to start calling her Mum, don't you think?' She shrugged, as if it didn't matter. 'She asked me to call her that.'

'It suits her,' he said, taking her arm as they headed for the door.

She stiffened momentarily, then forced herself to relax. If she pulled away, he'd think that what he said, did, mattered to her.

'What's that supposed to mean?' she asked, once they were outside, but keeping her voice light.

He held up his hands in mock surrender. 'She's classy.'

'Not quite the same thing.'

'What can I say? She's a real head-turner, Lou.' Then, with a wry grin, 'Don't let her near my father. He has a fatal weakness for that chorus-girl-fallen-on-good-times look.'

'Your father has a fatal weakness for women full-stop.'

'Life has never been dull,' he agreed, and it was Louise who found herself reaching out to him, tucking her arm through his as they walked away from the square. 'I don't think you understand how lucky you've been. How much I envied you the sheer ordinariness of your family.'

'Ordinariness?'

'It's what boys yearn for. Parents who don't attract attention.'

'Oh, dear. Bad luck,' she said, laughing. 'How is Aunt Georgina? Where is she?'

'In Mexico, painting up a storm. Apparently the light is magical. She's living with someone called Jose who's half her age.' He looked at her. 'Ring

Ivy, Louise. Don't abandon something precious to chase rainbows.'

She shook her head. Unwilling to admit that he was right. But Max had been no more than a toddler when his parents had split up. Since then there had been a succession of stepmothers, half-siblings, step-siblings from his father. Drama and lovers from his mother. No one, she thought, had ever put Max first. It was scarcely any wonder that he had given all his heart, his loyalty to the business. Bella Lucia had never hurt him.

She looked up, but not far; in her high heels her eyes were nearly on a level with his.

'I will call her,' she promised.

'When?'

'Soon.' Then, because all that hurt too much to think about, 'Chorus girl fallen on good times?'

'The glamour, the clothes, the diamonds in those rings…'

'So what you're saying is that she's a classy "broad" rather than a product of the finishing school, debutante system? Now I'm afraid to ask what I owe to nature as opposed to nurture.'

It was the height of the rush-hour and Max, sensing approaching quicksand, used the excuse of looking around for a cruising cab to avoid her direct gaze.

'Well?' she demanded.

'I thought you didn't want to know.'

'Oh, please…'

'It's not something I could put into words,' he said.

How could you possibly quantify the smoke and mirrors of sex appeal? Pin it down, list the components. Item: hair, the colour of ripe wheat rippling in the wind. Item: two eyes, blue-grey, unless she was angry, when they were like storm clouds threaded with lightning. Item: one mouth…

He found himself staring at her mouth. Parted slightly, as if she were on the point of saying something outrageous. On the point of laughing. Dark, rich, enticing. The colour of the small sweet plums he picked in his Italian grandmother's family home on rare and treasured holidays, when he'd been taken along to keep his half-brother Jack from getting into mischief. To give his father time to spend with wife number three…

'Do you think there's any chance we'll find a taxi at this time of day?' he asked, abruptly.

She lifted a hand and, as if by magic, a black cab materialised alongside them.

'Where are we going?' she asked as he opened the door.

We? That was promising.

'Mayfair. My office,' he said, taking advantage of the opportunity she'd given him. 'I'm going to make you an offer you can't refuse.'

'Oh, this should be good,' she said, climbing in without argument.

Something of a first, that, but he was too busy enjoying the view to comment on it. Item: one pair of finely boned ankles that drew the eye upwards in an appreciation of her long legs…

Pulling himself together, he told the driver to take them to Berkeley Square, the home of the Mayfair Bella Lucia and the company offices, and then climbed in beside her.

She was glowing, he thought. Happy. A transformation from her arrival at the gallery. She hadn't seen him, but he'd arrived before her, seen how tense she'd looked. The meeting with her mother had gone well. Maybe that was a good thing. Patsy lived in London…

'What do you think it will take?' she asked, breaking into his thoughts.

'Sorry?'

'I'm interested in what you believe you'll have to offer, before I can't refuse?'

'If I told you that, you'd know more than I do.'

'No, Max. I already know what it'll take. You're the one who has to find the perfect combination.' She was smiling, but her face offered no clues. 'I hope you've got nothing else planned for the rest of the evening.'

He tried to forget the mountain of paperwork on his desk as he said, 'I cleared my diary. I've got as long as it takes.'

To say that her expression changed would have been an exaggeration, but for a split second he thought he'd found the key. Then, she glanced out of the window, as if the passing traffic was of more interest than anything he had to offer. Then, 'Try, Max.'

'Try?' he repeated, confused. She wanted him to open negotiations here, in the back of a taxi?

'To put it into words. What I owe to Patsy.' She turned to face him. 'What I owe to nature.'

He had the uncomfortable feeling that she was playing with him. That she knew exactly what she wanted and that when she was ready she would tell him; in the meantime she was enjoying making him sweat a little.

'Sorry, Lou,' he said. 'I have an aversion to having my face slapped.'

'I would never slap your face, Max.' Her lashes swept down as she did her best to hide a satisfied little smile, demonstrating beyond any doubt that sex appeal was so much more than the sum of its parts. Describing it was like trying to catch mist. Or trying to explain a smile when the difference between the mechanics—some magic movement of muscles that lifted the mouth and went all the way up to the eyes—and the combined effect were so utterly indescribable...

'You were quite prepared to throw a fully loaded vase at my head,' he reminded her.

'That was a long time ago, Max. And I didn't actually hit you.'

'Only because your aim was so lousy. As it was you wrecked the table behind me. Dinner and dry-cleaning bills on the house, for eight.'

'I'm surprised you didn't deduct the cost from my wages when you fired me.'

'My mistake. Dad took the damage out of mine.'

She shook her head, biting on her lower lip to stop herself from laughing. He couldn't take his eyes off it. He wanted to tell her to stop, pull her lip free, kiss it, bite it…

'I'm sorry.'

'Believe me, it was worth every penny to get you out of my hair.'

'Careful, Max…'

'You were a terrible *maître d'*, Louise. Be honest. I did you a favour.'

She smiled. 'Yes, I suppose you did.' Then, 'I can't even remember what you said that made me so mad.'

'Everything I said made you mad.'

'True.' Suddenly sobered, she said, 'So why are you so anxious to have me come and work for you?'

Because he was crazy, he thought.

They didn't have a problem? Who did he think he was kidding? Working with Louise was going to try his self-control to the limits.

He took a slow breath.

'I want you to work *with* me, Lou, not *for* me. I respect your skill, your judgement, but we both know that I could buy that out in the marketplace. What makes you special, unique, is that you've spent a lifetime breathing in the very essence of Bella Lucia. You're a Valentine to your fingertips, Louise; the fact that you're adopted doesn't alter any of that.'

'It alters how I feel.'

'I understand that and, for what it's worth, I think Ivy and John were wrong not to tell you the truth, but it doesn't change who or what you are. Jack wants you on board, Louise, and he's right.'

'He's been chasing you? Wants to know why you haven't signed me up yet? Well, that would explain your sudden enthusiasm.'

'He wanted to know the situation before he took off last week.'

'Took off? Where's he gone?'

'He was planning to meet up with Maddie in Florence at the weekend. To propose to her.'

'You're kidding!' Then, when he shook his head, 'Oh, but that's so romantic!' Then, apparently recalling the way he'd flirted with Maddie at the Christmas party, she said, 'Are you okay with that?'

He found her concern unexpectedly touching. 'More than okay,' he assured her. 'I was only winding Jack up at Christmas. It's what brothers do.' His first reaction when Jack had tossed Louise in his lap had been to assume that it was tit for tat.

'You must have really put the wind up him if he was driven to marriage,' she said.

'Bearing in mind our father's poor example, I think you can be sure that he wouldn't have married her unless he loved her, Lou.'

Or was he speaking for himself?

'No. Of course not. I'm sorry.'

Sorry? Louise apologising to him? That had to be a first. Things were looking up.

She laughed.

'What?'

She shook her head. 'Weddings to the left of us, weddings to the right of us and not one of them held at a family restaurant.' She tutted. 'You know what you need, Max? Some heavyweight marketing muscle.'

'I'm only interested in the best, Louise so why don't we stop pussyfooting around, wasting time when we could be planning for the future?' The thought of an entire evening with her teasing him, drawing out concessions one by one, exacting repayment for every time he'd let her down, every humiliation, was enough to bring him out in a cold sweat. 'Why don't you tell me what it's going to cost me? Your bottom line.'

'You don't want to haggle?'

Definitely teasing.

'You want to see me suffer, is that it? If I call it total surrender, will that satisfy your injured pride?'

Her smile was as enigmatic as anything the Mona Lisa could offer. 'Total surrender might be acceptable,' she told him.

'You've got it. So, what's your price?'

'Nothing.'

He stared at her, shocked out of teasing. That was it? A cold refusal?

'Nothing?' Then, when she didn't deny it, 'You mean that this has all been some kind of elaborate wind-up? That you're not even going to consider my proposal?'

'As a proposal it lacked certain elements.'

'Money? You know what you're worth, Louise. We're not going to quibble over a consultancy fee.'

She shook her head. 'No fee.'

Outside the taxi the world moved on, busy, noisy. Commuters crossing *en masse* at the lights, the heavy diesel engine of a bus in the next lane, a distant siren. Inside it was still, silent, as if the world were holding its breath.

'No fee?' he repeated.

'I'll do what you want, Max. I'll give you—give the family—my time. It won't cost you a penny.'

He didn't fall for it. Nothing came without some cost.

'You can't work without being paid, Louise.'

'It's not going to be for ever. I'll give you my time until…until the fourteenth. Valentine's Day. The diamond anniversary of the founding of Bella Lucia.'

'Three weeks. Is that all?'

'It's all I can spare. My reward is my freedom, Max. I owe the family and I'll do this for them. Then the slate will be wiped clean.'

'No…'

He didn't like the sound of that. He didn't want her for just a few weeks. Didn't want to be treated like a client, even if he was getting her time for free. Having fought the idea for so long, he discovered that he wanted more, a lot more from her than that.

'You're wrong. You can't just walk away, replace one family with another. You can't wipe away a lifetime of memories, of care—'

'It's the best deal you're ever likely to get,' she said, cutting him short before he could add, '…of love…'

'Even so. I can't accept it.'

'You don't have a choice,' she said. 'You asked for my bottom line; that's it.'

'There's always a choice,' he said, determined that she shouldn't back him into a corner, use Bella Lucia as a salve to her conscience, so that she could walk away without a backward glance. Something that he knew she'd come to regret.

Forget Bella Lucia.

This was more important and, if he did nothing else, he had to stop her from throwing away something so precious.

'That's my offer, Max. Take it or leave it.'

'There must be something that you want, that I can offer you,' he said, assailed by a gut-deep certainty that he must get her to accept something from them—from him. Make it more than a one-way transaction. For her sake as much as his. 'Not money,' he said, quickly, 'if that's the way you want it, but a token.'

'A token? Anything?'

Her eyes were leaden in the subdued light of the cab, impossible to read what she was thinking. That had changed. There had been a time when every thought had been written across her face, as easy to read as a book.

He was going into this blind.

'Anything,' he said.

'You insist?'

He nodded once.

'Then my fee for working with you on the expansion of the Bella Lucia restaurant group, Max, is a kiss.'

CHAPTER FOUR

MAX heard the words, struggled to make sense of them.

'A kiss?' What the hell…? What kind of a kiss? 'Just one?'

'Just one,' Louise replied.

Even in his head words failed him.

He was being choked by a collar and tie that were suddenly too tight. He fought the urge to loosen them. This was a game. He might not have been able to read her mind, but she'd clearly been reading his.

And now she was asking for the very thing he'd been resisting with every fibre of his being. Teasing him. Raising the stakes…

She was so *hot* in that sexy little suit, those high heels. Her hair curled in soft wisps around her face that seemed to direct his gaze directly to a mouth that was pure temptation and, given the fact that he'd been fighting the urge to kiss her, and more, for as long as he could remember, his sudden reluctance to comply with her simple request was hard to explain. Except that a kiss fallen into in the heat of desire, or passion or even simple lust, was one thing. But this cool, dispassionate proposition was something else.

It couldn't be that easy...

'Now?' he asked, doing his best to match her composure.

'You're in a hurry to seal the contract?'

Not just teasing but taunting him...

Or was that disappointment at his obvious lack of enthusiasm?

'It's your call,' he said, a touch hoarsely.

'Okay.'

Was that 'okay' now? Or 'okay' she'd leave it up to him?

She waited, offering no help, not coming an inch to meet him halfway.

Oh, hell...

Feeling very much like a teenager faced with his first real kiss, unsure quite what was expected of him, what 'a kiss' in this context entailed, heartily wishing he hadn't leapt in, said the first word that came into his head. "*Now...?*"

But she was waiting, eyes wide open, while he hovered on the brink of insanity, torn between an urgent need to go for the straight-to-hell moment he'd been fighting all his life and the suspicion that she was somehow testing him, making certain that they could work together, that he could control himself. That she could control herself.

As he hesitated between heaven and hell the taxi swung around the corner, throwing her off balance, so that instead of kissing her he had an armful of her when they came to a halt in front of the restaurant.

An armful of the softest, sexiest woman a man could imagine only in his wildest dreams. Delivering on those dreams—or were they nightmares?—that had haunted him, souring every other relationship, until he'd finally stopped trying to find someone who could drive her from his thoughts and done what he'd always done, thrown himself heart and soul into work, turning to the one thing in his life that had always been there, never let him down.

Bella Lucia.

She didn't move and it was all he could do not to deliver with the kind of kiss that she would regret calling down on her head. Not some polite token that would torment his soul, surely her intention, but a kiss that would mark her as his with the kind of pledge that would seal their alliance for eternity.

The driver leaned back and opened the door when they didn't move and he realised with relief that there was someone waiting to grab the cab. That time had run out.

'Bad...' His voice caught in his throat. 'Bad timing...' he said.

'Maybe,' she said, so softly that she was almost inaudible. Then, before he could do or say anything, she extricated herself from his arms, climbed out onto the pavement, walked towards the restaurant without looking back.

'You all right, guv?' the driver asked as, hands shaking, he handed over the fare.

'Fine,' he said, abruptly. There was nothing wrong with him that a long, cold shower wouldn't fix. 'We should have been wearing seat belts. Keep the change.'

The discreet façade of the Berkeley Square Bella Lucia fronted one of London's most exclusive, most luxurious restaurants, a place where financiers, politicians, the world's deal brokers came to meet, eat and talk, confident of their privacy in the gentlemen's club atmosphere.

Louise regarded it with every appearance of composure, even though she was trembling, holding herself together through sheer will power despite the sudden urge to bolt.

Performance nerves, that was all.

She knew how to use the adrenalin rush to see her through big presentations, major launches. When it came to business she had no trouble keeping her feelings under wraps and she could do it now. Except that hadn't been about business.

She didn't know what it had been about except that Max had been pushing her and as always she'd responded with a reckless disregard for the consequences.

She turned as he joined her, smiled distantly, still performing as he wordlessly held the door. She walked ahead of him through the panelled, ground floor entrance, across the small bar with its comfortable leather chairs where the staff were already preparing for the evening, into the restaurant, aware all the time of the heat of his arm, not quite touching, at her back. Still feeling the pressure where he'd caught her, held her.

'I've always loved this moment,' she said, calling on every reserve of control to act as if nothing had happened. Using the excuse to stop, rest her hands lightly on the back of a chair as her legs began to wobble dangerously. Looking around. Anywhere but at him.

'Pure theatre,' Max agreed, without having to ask what she meant. He knew.

Behind the scenes, in the kitchen, the food was being prepared, the front of house staff were assembling. Out here the tables were laid with snowy white cloths, polished silver, glasses, fresh flowers.

Not just theatre, she thought, but the grandest of opera, everything was ready, waiting for the audience to appear, for the conductor to raise his baton and the evening to begin.

Until a few months ago that had been her father. This restaurant, the smaller private dining rooms on the floor above, the offices on the top floor, had been the heart from which he'd run the Bella Lucia empire.

'He nearly lost it,' she said, more to herself than Max, using anger to drive off the intensity of that moment in the taxi. She was angry, she realised, because of all of them Max would have been the one who lost most. Perhaps everything… 'All for the sake of a son he hadn't known existed until a few months ago.'

'He'd have done the same for you, Louise.'

Would he?

When Daniel and Dominic had turned up, twin images of John Valentine, saying 'Hi, Dad…' they'd been received like prodigal sons by John, while her reward for thirty-something years of dutiful daughterhood had been the shocking revelation that she was not actually Ivy and John's daughter at all, but had been adopted at birth.

She'd suddenly felt invisible, excluded.

Blood was thicker…

'He wouldn't have had to,' she said, keeping her voice even, matter-of-fact.

Easy for you to say, the still small voice of her conscience reminded her. John Valentine would have given you anything. Has given you everything…

Which was why she was here now. Paying her dues.

'Forget the past, Louise,' Max said, catching her hand, holding it, forcing her to look at him. 'Bella Lucia is still here. We're still here. It's the future that matters.' His hand tightened around hers as if he could somehow transmit his excitement to her by direct contact. 'Expanding. The new restaurant in Qu'Arim is just the beginning. I'm going to launch the third generation of Bella Lucia onto a world stage. Close your eyes, stick a pin in a map and ten years from now we'll be there. Don't you want to be a part of that?'

No! Yes…

All her life, ever since she was a little girl, she'd longed to be here, centre stage. Back then her dream had been to be at her father's side, but Max—older, male, the first-born Valentine grandson—had always been ahead of her.

Now he needed her he was using family ties to draw her back into the business, but it would always be his empire. She would always come second. Second to her father was the way of the world, she could have lived with that; second to Max was never going to be enough.

Why did it have to be him?

Because it was his life, she thought, answering her own question. He loved it. He was like his father in that, if in nothing else.

The staff had always trusted him, turned to him. Even now he was doing this as much for them as for himself. They were, she realised, his family. Which was why she'd do her best to help him put Bella Lucia on the world map.

She'd do it for him, for her father, for the Valentine family that she'd always thought she was a part of. And for herself, too, so that she could walk away with a clear conscience. All debts paid. But she would walk away…

'Lou?' He was pressing her to commit. To say the word.

'Yes,' she said, as matter-of-factly as if he'd asked her if she wanted a drink.

Her answer was always going to be, had to be, yes.

For now. Until the fourteenth of February. Valentine's Day.

'What's the matter? You don't look convinced?' She let loose a smile that was trying to break out. 'You did say that you wouldn't take no for an answer.'

For once Max seemed lost for words, a predicament so rare that she'd have to be a saint not to take some pleasure from the situation. The truth was that all day she'd been on pins, nervous about meeting her mother for the first time, nerves that had been made worse by the background tension: her cast-iron certainty that Max was simply going through the motions to convince Jack that he had done all he could to bring her on board. That he didn't really want her.

But the meeting with her mother had gone better than she could ever have imagined and then, when she'd seen Max waiting for her at the gallery, that for once he'd kept his promise, made time for her…

She didn't, in her heart of hearts, believe that anything other than desperation would have driven him to make such a gesture, but he had made it, demonstrating beyond words that she was the one in the driving seat. That he needed her, that the family was relying on her. Taking her seriously for once.

How could she not say 'yes'?

'For the moment my time is completely booked up with the relaunch of HOTfood, but once that's out of the way—'

'When?' he demanded, impatiently. 'When can you start?'

'After the party on Friday.' She looked up at him. 'After that I'll be all yours.'

It was only when she wanted to tuck a loose strand of hair behind her ear that she realised Max was still holding her hand, and as she looked up at him she found herself remembering years before when, on a family trip to the beach, he'd reached out to her when she couldn't keep up with him and Jack as they'd scrambled over the rocks.

How he'd stopped, come back to hold out a hand to her. How safe she'd felt.

Remembering how safe she'd always felt. How lucky she'd been...

'You haven't got a fistful of clients hammering on your door?' he asked, abruptly abandoning her hand to straighten a fork on the table.

'What? Oh, yes. Well, actually, no...' She tucked back her hair, said, 'I haven't taken on any new jobs since my return from Australia. I didn't want to tie myself down.'

He frowned. 'You were really serious about leaving?'

Was she?

In truth she hadn't known. It was as if she'd been poised between her old life and the possibility of something new, waiting for some small sign to set her on the right path.

What she'd got, in the shape of Max Valentine, was a three-lane motorway direction sign saying 'BELLA LUCIA'...

His question suggested that as far as he was concerned it was a momentary whim to be brushed aside now she was back in the fold and, deciding that it was wiser to leave him with that impression, she lifted her shoulders in a wordless shrug.

He let it go, said, 'I didn't ask if you were free this evening.'

'No, you didn't.'

'Are you?'

There were two possible answers to that question.

One… She could tell him that she had to work and then waste the evening pointlessly stressing over the last minute details of the HOTfood party even though she knew there was nothing left to do, or…

Two… 'No, Max. I'm not free. I'm having a working supper with the new head of the Valentine empire. Unless you've got something more interesting planned?'

His response was a sudden smile that involved every part of his face, deepening the creases that bracketed his mouth, lighting up his eyes in a way that almost impossibly intensified the blue. The kind that took time, that she hadn't seen in years.

'I can't think of anything more interesting than that,' he said and she was forced to bludgeon down the heart leap, the foolish warmth at his admission that being with her would be a pleasure rather than a pain.

'Interesting' was what he'd actually said.

In some cultures 'interesting' was a curse…

'If that's your measure of interesting, Max,' she

replied, 'you need to put some serious thought into getting a life.'

He looked as if he was about to say something. He clearly thought better of it, because instead he shrugged, said, 'This *is* my life.'

He'd got that right, anyway. The restaurants, the people who worked for them; he'd strived for success not just for himself, the family, but because he knew that it was the men and women who worked for them who would suffer most if things went wrong.

He'd only fired her, she realised, because her volatility when she was around him threatened that success…

'Come on, let's get started,' he said, ignoring the lift in favour of the stairs. 'I've been thinking about some of your ideas.'

'Which ones?' she asked, taking them rather more sedately in her high heels and narrow skirt.

'All of them, but especially Meridia. I really think you're on to something so I sent Emma an email and asked her to look out for likely locations.'

'Your sister doesn't work for you any more, Max,' she reminded him. 'In fact I imagine being Queen of Meridia doesn't leave her with too much spare time to spend running errands for you.'

'You think?'

He stopped without warning, turned and, a step

below him, she was suddenly cheek-to-chest close. Without thinking she swayed back to avoid touching him, just as she always had, just as he always had, but now he put out a hand to grab her, steady her as she took a step back. Save her from a fall. Keep her close.

'If we're not cousins,' he'd said, 'we don't have a problem...'

Not for him, maybe, but it was as if that moment when he'd come close to kissing her had intensified her response to him. Even through her coat, the sleeve of her suit, his hand was applying heat to a square of skin just above her elbow that spread like wildfire to every part of her body.

Just the simple act of breathing became suddenly more difficult.

Yes...

The word whispered through her mind, silken temptation.

This was what you wanted. Max at your feet. Max in your bed...

'Yes,' she said. Then, when he waited for her to elaborate. 'I do think.'

'Well, never mind,' he said, with a tormenting smile that she knew only too well, 'I've got you for that now.'

Got her? To run his errands? Was that what he thought? Not even close...

'You think?' she enquired, throwing his words back at him as the heat intensified to a dangerous calm. She knew this feeling, recognised this, welcomed it even; the motorway sign was flashing an urgent warning 'SLOW — ACCIDENT AHEAD' but, just as she always had, she ignored it.

'What are you looking for?' Max asked as she cast about her before fixing her gaze on the vast arrangement of flowers on the half landing where the staircase split into two and curved away on either side.

She blinked, collected herself, swallowed.

What was she thinking? She was grown up, an in-demand consultant, not some stupid girl with a crush.

Get a grip. He was just teasing.

There had been a time when his teasing had made her insides curl up in a paroxysm of pleasure that this godlike figure had noticed her.

A lifetime ago.

Then there had come a time when it had just made her mad.

Now…

'A vase,' she said. 'If you think I'm interested in running your errands, Max, you obviously need a large dose of cold water.'

For a moment he just stood there and she knew, just knew, that it was going to be a rerun of the last time they'd worked together; he said something dumb, she responded like an outraged cat, spitting and arching her back, then he blew up.

And she felt nothing but regret.

'Since your aim is as bad as your timing,' he said, after a monumental pause that had probably been no more than a heartbeat but which had seemed to stretch for a hundred years, 'maybe we should take the cold shower as read.'

Her timing?

'My timing is off? I like that! You were the one who couldn't wait. One kiss, a token, how hard could that be?'

No! No... Do not remind him of that foolishness...

'My mistake. Just tell me when and we'll seal the contract.'

Tell him it was a joke. That you didn't mean it... Now!

But her gaze was riveted to his mouth, her own lips burning with a lifetime of unrequited longing, of denial, and with her breath caught in her throat she was unable to speak.

'Your call,' he prompted, clearly in no hurry.

It was enough to break the spell. With extreme care, she said, 'Thanks. I'll let you know.'

'Any time,' he said, then turned away before she could respond, taking the rest of the stairs in a couple of strides.

By the time she'd caught up with him on the top

floor where the offices were situated she'd recovered her composure, had reminded herself that this was supposed to be a working supper. Posted a mental note to keep a curb on her tongue.

It would probably get easier with practice.

In the meantime, Meridia.

'Are you—we—doing the catering for this big gala dinner and ball Emma is throwing to launch her "Queen's Charity"?' she asked, focussing on business.

'I'm signing the contract on Monday. Do you want to come?'

'To the ball?'

Was he asking her…?

'I imagine Emma will want you there.' Then, as she hesitated, 'She adores you, Louise.' Oh, right, just more propaganda on behalf of the family.

'Of course I'll go,' she said. 'Who in their right mind would give up a chance to buy a new dress?'

Most people would have taken her response at face value. The look Max gave her suggested that he was not so easily fooled.

'All right, Max. I'll be there for her.'

Just for Emma.

After a moment he nodded, accepting that she was sincere. It was frightening how easily he could read her.

'Good. But I was asking if you want to come with me to Meridia on Monday.'

'Oh, I see.'

It was unnerving how much she'd wanted him to be asking her to the ball as his partner. Still sixteen and waiting for her prom night Prince Charming. Still yearning to feel his arms around her. Instead she got a business meeting…

'Well, it would be useful.' Then, forcing herself to keep to the point, 'Actually, since we're doing the catering I'd like to discuss the possibility of a behind-the-scenes-in-the-palace-kitchens feature with the royal PR people. The work involved in putting on a royal gala ball. If you're serious about moving into Meridia—'

'I'm serious. You're right; it's the obvious place to start.'

'Then the "Queen's Charity" tie-in would be exactly the moment to announce the fact.'

'Hold on. It's a little premature to be thinking that far ahead.'

'It's never too soon for thought, Max. You have to take advantage of media at the moment when they want something from you.' She saw his doubt. 'It's not until June and the feature wouldn't appear until the week of the gala. You can drop the news into an interview I'll set up for you to talk about that. That's if you're serious—'

'I told you I'm serious!'

'Good,' she said. 'Good. Then we need to make

the most of the moment, ride on the coat tails of the publicity that will generate. Whatever happens, the royal connection will add lustre to the outside-event catering side of the business.'

He still looked doubtful. 'Do you really think Sebastian will allow photographers, journalists, to roam loose in the palace? Isn't there a danger that we'll be perceived as using our royal connection for commercial gain? I'm concerned it will hurt Emma.'

'Just the kitchens, a glimpse of the food we'll be serving—we can photograph that here. Some behind-the-scenes pictures of the banqueting room being made ready would be good, but since that's already part of the tour visitors can take it's hardly likely to prove a problem.' He didn't look convinced. 'Sebastian will want publicity for the charity and it's the charity I'll focus on. Obviously the copyright of the photographs would be invested in that. The major lifestyle magazines will pay huge money for a royal feature like this.'

'You've been giving this a lot of thought.'

'This is PR 101, Max. Sebastian's a modern monarch. He knows he's going to have to sell his country to tourists, industrialists, bankers. Put together royalty and romance with fabulous food and you have an unbeatable combination. Add a charming young queen launching a charity to help the world's poor and Meridia is the winner.'

He glanced at his watch. 'Five minutes. You've come up with all that in five minutes?'

'That's just the thinking. I still have to make the connections, set up the deal. Do the work.' She managed a smile. 'I'm going to need every minute of that three weeks.' Then, before he could press her for more, 'We'll all be winners, Max. And besides, I won't have to persuade Sebastian,' she added. 'That is one job I'm happy to leave in the capable hands of your little sister. She owes me.'

'For transforming her from a rather plain duckling into a stunning swan?'

'Emma isn't plain,' she said, scolding him. 'Far from it. She just needed a little help with her confidence; all I did was bring out the inner princess.' Then, unable to resist fishing for a compliment from him, 'You noticed how lovely she looked?'

'When Sebastian introduced her as his future queen at his coronation the entire world noticed. You did a great job.'

'She was such a beautiful bride,' she said, unable to resist a little sigh of satisfaction, not just because her efforts had been so amply rewarded, but that Max had been generous enough to credit her with the transformation.

'It's what you do, isn't it?' he said. 'Make people take notice. Create an image.'

'More than an image, Max. My job is to create a

feeling, an "I want" response, to choreograph a reflection in words and pictures that reinforce the desire so that when anyone thinks of the ultimate in a rare, luxurious dining experience, anywhere in the world, the first name that comes to mind is Bella Lucia.'

'Can you really do that?'

'I'll give it my best shot.' Then, feeling a little self-conscious at having made a pitch to someone she'd known all her life, she turned away, indicated his laptop. 'Can I borrow that to go online, do a little research?'

'Now?'

She stopped, looked at him. 'Is that your stock answer, Max?' Then, quickly, 'Yes, now.'

'I thought…'

'What? That we were just going to have another cosy supper?' Hadn't he learned from what had happened yesterday? 'When I say I'm having a working supper, I mean *working*. Since you appear to be more interested in the supper, I'll leave you to organise that.'

'Thanks,' he said, drily. 'Actually, I have got a pile of work to catch up with so I'll need the laptop, but you could use the machine in your father's old office,' he said, leading the way. 'You'll probably want to upgrade it. Have the whole office redecorated if you like. Buy some new furniture.'

'Why would I want to do that?' she asked,

walking through the door, touching her father's desk, slipping into his huge leather chair, remembering the times she'd begged to stay with him when her mother had dropped in after shopping, for coffee, lunch.

How she'd climbed onto his lap, drawing pictures while he'd worked, nibbling on the little savoury treats he'd had sent up for her from the kitchen. Both of them getting a ticking off from her mother for spoiling her appetite…

'For three weeks,' she added, pushing the memory away. Except, of course, they both knew he wanted more than that. 'I've got state-of-the-art equipment in my own office,' she said.

And suddenly she had his full attention.

'I thought…'

She knew what he thought. That she'd move in here while she worked on the Bella Lucia account and in one bound he'd have her back in the family fold.

'Just so you know, so that there are no misunderstandings, Max, what you're getting from me is a marketing plan. An image. Some publicity. Some ideas. You're not getting my business, my life or anything else.'

Not for a kiss.

Max watched as she switched on the computer, absently tucking a strand of hair behind her ear as the machine booted up, concentrating on the screen as she logged onto the internet. For a moment he thought that she'd forgotten him, but then she glanced up as if surprised to still see him there, before her attention was reclaimed by the computer and she turned back to the screen.

He returned to his own office, sat at his desk, trying to work out whether he'd got what he wanted, or whether it was Louise who was calling all the shots. True, she was working with him, but very much on her own terms, in her own office. That wasn't what he'd envisaged. What he'd wanted.

What did he want?

His plans were huge and he'd never doubted his ability to put them into action; he'd got that drive from his father. He'd been less than thrilled with Jack when he'd suggested he needed Louise. But it had been impossible to avoid the fact that the world had felt a very lonely place as he'd stepped up to take sole responsibility for Bella Lucia, all the people who worked for him relying on him to make the money that paid their mortgages, for their children's shoes.

Knowing that they were going to be in this together, made the whole thing so much more… What? He sifted through the words that offered themselves. Satisfying. Pleasing. Enjoyable… No, more than that. And as the right word dropped into his mind he grinned.

Fun.

It had stopped feeling like the weight of the world on his shoulders and had started to feel like an adventure.

And there was still the kiss to look forward to, he thought, smiling as he reached for the stack of paperwork.

He was deeply absorbed in the quotations for a re-decoration of one of the Mayfair dining rooms when Martin, a waiter who'd been with them for years, arrived with a tray and began to lay the small dining table in the corner of his office. He glanced at his watch, saw that it was nearly nine.

'I hadn't realised it was so late.'

'Miss Valentine rang through to the kitchen to see if you'd ordered anything. I offered to bring up a menu, but she just asked for the mushroom risotto.'

'For both of us?'

'I could ask Chef for something else if you'd prefer?' Martin said, catching his initial irritation at not being consulted, but unable to feel the almost instant follow-up of something much nearer pleasure that she already felt sufficiently at ease, at home, to call down and order food.

Maybe, he thought, that was the way to do it. If he stopped pushing so hard, she'd relax, come back in from the cold without even noticing she was doing it.

'The risotto will be fine, Martin. Did she choose a wine?'

'No, sir.'

'Ask Georges for a bottle of Krug, will you?'

'Krug?' the waiter repeated. It wasn't something he'd want to make a mistake about.

'A small celebration. Miss Valentine is going to be working with us for a few weeks.'

'I'm delighted to hear it, sir.'

A few minutes later, having asked Martin to give him ten minutes before he brought up the food, he walked through to the other office, bearing two glasses of champagne.

'Supper's on its way up,' he said. Absorbed in what she was doing, Louise raised a hand to indicate that she'd heard him and carried on working. He set down the glasses and joined her behind the desk interested to see what she was doing. 'Is that Meridia?' he asked, leaning over her shoulder to look at an aerial photograph of a small island, surmounted by an equally small castle.

'I downloaded Google Earth so that I could take a close look at the capital, refresh my memory of the layout. And then I remembered this,' she said, using the mouse to fly them in over the island, before moving lower, taking him on an aerial tour around the castle. 'Do you see?'

'Very pretty. So?'

'It's a fishing lodge that belongs to some distant cousin of Sebastian's. Emma told me about it. He's a bit of a black sheep, apparently; *persona non grata* in the country. It's got a natural harbour, a small beach...'

'So?'

She turned and looked up at him, clearly expecting a response. 'So, it would make a perfect setting for a Bella Lucia restaurant,' she said, her eyes sparkling with an infectious enthusiasm that sent a charge of recognition skipping through him. She was, he thought, as excited by all this as he was.

'I can certainly see the attraction, but unless the man is looking for a tenant...'

'Well, he can't use it himself. I called Emma to run the idea past her and ask if there was any possibility of us looking at the place when we're there on Monday. It's all fixed.'

He frowned. 'Oh, come on, it can't be that easy...' Then, 'You're serious?'

'Of course. I don't have time to mess about. Oh, and I've arranged for us to meet with the director of the State Tourism Office, too.'

'You seem to have organised everything.' He straightened, no longer smiling. 'Are you sure you need me to come with you?'

'I'm sorry, Max?' she said, instantly catching the change in his mood.

She said it not as if she were truly sorry, or actually thought she might have overstepped some unseen line, but as if he were the one in the wrong.

'The words "bull" and "china shop" leap to mind. There's a fine difference between being keen,' he said, 'and rushing in without taking time to consider all the options.'

'I've suggested a location that I've already seen, I've arranged a viewing—using my personal contact with a queen, no less,' she pointed out, 'and I've organised a meeting with a man who would be useful in setting up a joint venture with a local hotelier, since—and correct me if I'm wrong—I assume you don't have any plans to move into the hotel business, too.' She paused for half a beat, then said, 'What have you done in the last couple of hours?'

'Cleared a mountain of paperwork I should have been attending to this afternoon instead of hanging around the Portrait Gallery waiting for you,' he said. 'This company doesn't run itself, you know.'

'Nobody asked you,' she reminded him. 'I didn't need you. You were the one who insisted, wanted to show how much you care about me—'

'I do, Louise. We all do.'

'Please! What you want is for me to play happy families, come and work for you, and now you think you've got all that, it's as you were. Well, if this is going to be the kind of "working together"…' and she did that really irritating quotes thing again, presumably with the precise intention of irritating him '…where I'm supposed to stand on the sidelines making suggestions while you make all the decisions, sorry, but I'm not interested.'

'This is going to be a working relationship, Lou,' he said, holding onto his own temper by the skin of his teeth, 'where we discuss things, then we decide what to do, then we take action.'

'If I'd waited for you to order supper, we'd have starved,' she said, already beyond reason, but then her reaction to criticism had always been to over-react. The simplest thing had sent her overboard. A suggestion that her skirt was too short. A reprimand for flirting with the customers…

She was incapable of backing down, admitting a mistake.

'Dammit, Louise,' he said, 'you haven't changed one bit—'

'Dammit, Max, neither have you!' She was on her feet, in his face. 'You're still the same arrogant, overbearing, despotic, pigheaded idiot you always were!'

CHAPTER FIVE

LOUISE was outraged. He'd said this was what he'd wanted her for, but when she used her initiative, got on with the job, he couldn't handle it.

'Forget it, Max,' she said, reaching for her bag. 'This is never—'

'Don't!' He grabbed her by the shoulders before she could pick it up, spinning her around to face him. 'Don't say another word!'

'Never,' she repeated, blazing her defiance at him. 'Going—'

'Lou!' he warned.

'To—'

His mouth descended on hers with the impact of fire on ice, stopping her words, stopping her breath, stopping her heart.

For an instant the world was an explosion of hissing, sizzling reaction on the surface while inside she remained frozen with shock. Then his arms were around her, pulling her close and she was clinging to him as her lips, her bones, her brain were overwhelmed by the heat and began, very slowly, to melt.

This was it.

This was the moment she'd yearned for, struggled against all her adult life. To know this, feel this.

To taste Max on her lips, feel the silk of his tongue stopping her angry words, showing her that she wasn't alone. That he was suffering too...

Her arms wound themselves around his neck, her fingers made free with hair that she'd longed to touch, knowing in some dark corner of her mind that she'd wantonly engineered this, forced this moment.

She'd wanted this ever since that moment at the Valentine's Day party when, sixteen years old and full of herself, she'd grabbed his hand, insisting on teaching him the steps of the newest dance. And then, as the music had changed to something slower, she'd seen something shift in the way he was looking at her, seen his eyes darken and felt something new, something dangerous stir, respond, deep inside her, wanting a lot more.

She'd known, as he pulled away, that everything had changed between them. That a touch was no longer innocent. That even to look was an invitation that damned them both.

Young, angry, stupid, she'd pushed him and pushed him to take what she could see he wanted, what she wanted, even while she'd known it was forbidden, could never happen, until that final eruption when he'd sacked her, humiliated her, driven her so far away that there had been no way back.

She understood now that he'd been protecting himself, protecting both of them, in the only way he knew how.

But the day her father had told her she was adopted, all that had changed.

We don't have a problem…

He'd said it, but even then he'd held back, as if unable to overcome years of keeping the dark, unspoken need under tight control. Now, though, with his body hard against hers there could be no more pretence, no ignoring the truth between them. That she felt alive, wicked but alive as she never had before; knew that this was what she wanted, this was the token she'd demanded in return for coming back. Not just a kiss but his total surrender so that she could finally be free of the crippling desire for Max Valentine that had ruined every relationship she'd ever had.

Even as she clung to him he pulled back a little to look at her, his eyes dark, intense, yet giving nothing away, the habit of concealment too strong…

'You were saying?' he murmured, cool, self-possessed.

'I was?' Her body might be in flames, but she would match his cool… 'I don't recall,' she said, reclaiming her arms, understanding that, for now at least, the kiss was over.

Her composure would follow in its own good time.

His response was a slow, wide, seductive smile. 'Then I believe, we have a contract, Louise,' he said.

'You think?' she asked as he stepped back, picked up the glasses he'd brought with him. 'I don't believe I mentioned where exactly I wanted it. The kiss.'

She took the glass he was offering her before he actually spilled the contents, then continued, quite casually, 'You do know you're taking quite a risk giving me this? Track record would suggest that I'm as likely to toss it over you as drink it.'

'Maybe if I told you that it's Krug?' he offered.

'You think that would stop me?'

He managed a wry smile. 'On the contrary. I imagine it would add to your pleasure.'

Pleasure? There was no pleasure in it. In the past, when she'd thrown things, all she'd wanted was for him to stop saying things that made her angry, stop him criticising her, making her hate him.

'On the other hand, you do tend to respond in the heat of the moment. If you were going to throw it, you'd have done it already instead of talking about it.'

'True.' And besides, his way of putting a stop to a fight was so much more…interesting. 'If I've leapt in with both feet, Max, I'm sorry. I'm used to working on my own, not having to answer to anyone except the client.'

'I am the client.'

'So you are. My mistake.' She looked up, met his gaze directly then, with the smallest of shrugs, 'I may have got a little carried away in my excitement.' And he could take that any way he liked. 'Tomorrow I'll print out a note to stick on my computer—"TALK TO MAX".'

'Whilst I treasure the rarity of an apology from you, I suspect I'm the one who should be grovelling. This is what Jack wanted you on board for. Your quickness. Your vision. You weren't stepping on my toes, Louise. On the contrary, you were giving me a lift.' Then, 'Not that I'm trying to dissuade you from talking to me.'

Anything but, Max thought.

He'd kissed her because it had seemed the only way to stop her saying words that would have ended everything, to exert the control that was slipping away from him. He'd lost that the moment she'd begun to kiss him back. He was still numb with the shock of it; the only thing on his mind her scent, faint, seductive, making him want to pull her back into his arms, bury his face in her skin…

He was walking and talking as if nothing had happened, but inside he was in turmoil, only able to think of kissing her again, this time not for himself but for her.

Kissing her throat, her breasts, every inch of her until she was whimpering with pleasure, with need, so that they could finish what he'd started. Begin anew...

But he could never do that again. Next time it really would have to be her call, and she'd made it clear enough that she would call, that they had unfinished business. He could only hope that she wouldn't wait too long.

Even while he was sending urgent signals to his feet to step back, put a safe distance between them, she flipped her hair behind her ear out of the way in a give-away gesture that suddenly seemed as familiar to him as drawing breath.

She'd always done that, he realised, even when she was a little kid. When she was unsure of herself, out of her depth. Then, when she'd done it, she'd always looked at him for reassurance. Now she looked away.

'It might be a good idea to schedule a regular daily meeting,' she said, 'just to keep one another in the picture about what we're doing?'

Poised, composed, but now he knew it was all just an act. A very good one, to be sure, but it was no more than an ice glaze that hid a totally vulnerable core.

Beneath that apparent self-assurance her heart would be pounding, her mouth dry, her knees weak. He knew because that was the way he was feeling...

'What time would suit you best—morning or evening?' she prompted.

'The evening,' he said, without having to think about it. The evening offered all kinds of possibilities. A chat could become a drink, could become dinner, and after that anything was possible. 'Seven?' he suggested.

'Six-thirty would be better.' She waited, he had no choice but to nod. 'I'll slot half an hour into my diary.'

Not what he'd had in mind at all. But it was a start.

Her mouth lifted in a wry smile. 'Just listen to us, Max. Being so-o-o polite to each other. Who would have believed it possible?'

He forced a grin in response. 'Better make the most of it, Lou—it can't possibly last.'

'No.' For a moment they just looked at one another. 'But then who would want it to?' And he knew without doubt that she would call him on that kiss and when she did he'd better be ready to deliver everything she wanted.

The very thought almost fried his brains.

'You do realise that this job is going to take chunks out of any pretence at a personal life?' he said, making an effort to change the subject, but failing dismally.

'Is that why you can't keep a girl, Max?' she asked.

There was a time when that kind of remark would have brought him to the boil, hearing only the words, the implied criticism. Now all he heard was genuine concern.

'Relationships need time, hard work. You have to work at them if you want them to last.'

'No one has ever been that important to you?'

'Apparently not.' Then, because talking about his failures held no appeal, 'What happened to the Honourable James the gossip columnists had you all but down the aisle with a year or so back?'

'That was nearly three years ago.'

She reached for her hair again. Looked away. *No... Look at me...*

'As always,' she said, 'they mistook a light-hearted flirtation for something more important.'

About to suggest that it had looked a lot more than a light-hearted flirtation, he took pity on her. Whatever had gone wrong it was clearly still too raw to talk about and he was torn between a need to hit James Cadogan, and to wrap his arms around her and make it go away.

Since neither of the above was anything like a good idea, he settled for, 'There's a lot to be said for light-hearted flirtation when everyone knows the score.'

'My sentiments exactly, but then PR isn't exactly a nine-to-five job, either,' she said. 'In fact this is the only evening I've got free for the rest of the week.'

'Then it's a good thing I made an effort this afternoon.' And because he didn't want to remind her of all the times he hadn't made an effort, let her down, he raised his glass and said, 'A toast? To Bella Lucia. The future.'

By way of reply she lifted her glass, clinked it against his, said, '*Salute,* Max!'

Before he could reply, Martin tapped on the open office door. 'Your food is ready, Miss Valentine.'

'Thank you, Martin.' She made to move, then, when he didn't follow, 'Max? Risotto won't keep.'

But food was the last thing on his mind. She hadn't responded to his toast to the future of Bella Lucia, but had replied with the Italian equivalent of 'cheers'.

Louise was exhausted. Her feet ached; her head was pounding from music so loud she couldn't hear herself think. She'd spent the week not only orchestrating media involvement in the HOTfood launch, but clearing her desk of all the niggling little jobs that had to be done, leaving her free to concentrate on Bella Lucia. Free to fly to Meridia with Max after the weekend.

Max.

Their working supper had ended as soon as they'd

eaten. She'd made the excuse of an early start. He'd found her a taxi but it had taken all her powers of reasoning to dissuade him from escorting her home. By then she'd been desperate to get away from him, to clear her head, afraid that if he saw her to her door she'd drag him inside, tear his clothes off, tear her clothes off.

Distance didn't help.

Not even the coldest of showers could shift the memory of that kiss from her head. It was as if the lid had been lifted on desires she'd kept damped down for years and she'd got to the point where she was almost afraid to close her eyes, risk sleep, because when she slept she had no way of keeping them under control.

At least the week was over. Having spent what seemed like an endless evening at the HOTfood launch party the last thing she needed was to arrive home in the early hours of Saturday morning to find Cal Jameson camped out on her doorstep.

'All the hotels full?' she asked, irritably, as she fitted her key in the lock. Stupid question. Since his brother was now married to her half-sister, Cal apparently considered himself family. And family were put on earth to provide free food and accommodation whenever you were in town. Which, since Cal was in the travel business, was often.

Which was what you got when you took advantage of the innocent. She should never have fallen on his neck in gratitude when he'd obeyed her sister's orders and turned up at Christmas, blond, wide-shouldered and to die for in a perfectly cut dinner jacket, thus saving her from the embarrassment of arriving at the family party without a date.

Max always had some stunning eye-candy in tow and it was a matter of honour that she should match him, point-for-point, with the desirability of escort. Cal had delivered on appearance and that was all she'd asked for. She'd been away so much last year, had had so many other things on her mind, that she'd left it too late to round up a gallant willing to brave the Valentine family *en masse*.

When she'd seen that Max was on his own she'd felt a momentary pang of regret, but then he'd started flirting with Maddie, while she... She sighed. No use regretting what couldn't be changed.

'I left a message on your machine to say I had a stopover,' Cal said as he followed her upstairs like an eager puppy, totally oblivious to her lack of enthusiasm.

Maybe, she thought, she should send him over to Max, since he was so hot on the subject of family.

'When?' she asked.

'Just before I left Dubai. Don't ask me what time it was. I've crossed so many time zones in the last twenty-four hours I don't know what day it is.'

She didn't bother to enlighten him, but opened the door to her apartment, dropped the keys on the table, kicked off her shoes and tossed her coat over a chair. The red light on her answering machine was flashing, giving credence to his story. She ignored it.

'It wouldn't have made any difference what time you called. I haven't been home since six-thirty—'

'Jeez, Lou, what kind of bloke do you think I am?' She found the energy to raise an eyebrow. 'No, honestly,' he protested, 'it was earlier than that. You might have had a hot date or something.'

'It was the or something,' she assured him. 'When I said six-thirty, Cal, I meant six-thirty this morning.'

'You went to work dressed like that?'

He didn't wait for her denial, but whistled appreciatively at the clinging ankle-length dress she was wearing, chosen solely because it didn't wrinkle, even when it had spent all day rolled up in the bag she used to carry the essentials when she had to change on the job.

'You're welcome to stay,' she said, because he was family, sort of, 'but whatever you want, I'm afraid you're going to have to fend for yourself. I'm going to bed.'

'I'll take that,' he said, grinning broadly.

She finally cracked and laughed.

'No, really,' he assured her. 'I'm happy to share. I can see you're too tired to make up the spare bed.'

'In your dreams, Cal.'

'I've brought you a comfort package from Jodie,' he said, fishing out a padded envelope from his backpack.

'Jodie? How is she?' She missed her sister so much. Would phone her in the morning. 'And Heath?'

'Good.' Then, 'Double chocolate Tim Tams?' he said, waving the package temptingly in her direction.

'Really?' But no, she was not going to encourage him. 'Sorry, I've found a local supply.'

'You're kidding? Who'd have thought the Poms were that bright? What about DVDs of the latest episodes of *Beach Street*? I'll bet you can't get those two for the price of one at your local supermarket. Jodie tells me that you're an addict.'

While it was true that she had become... engaged...by one of the Aussie soaps while she was staying with her sister, she wasn't prepared to admit it.

'It's the spare room or nothing. If you want the bed made, you're going to have to do it yourself.'

'Fair enough,' he said, grinning. Totally un-ashamed. 'You can't blame a bloke for trying.'

Wrong bloke, she thought.

'You know the way, Cal. Don't disturb me before noon unless the building is on fire.'

* * *

An insistent ring on the doorbell dragged her from a dream in which Max had been kissing her. He'd started at her toes and it was just getting interesting... No, that was an understatement. It was already interesting. It was just getting...

'All right, all right...' she muttered as the doorbell rang again, pulling on a wrap, staggering to the door to press the intercom.

'Yes?'

'Louise, it's Max.'

'Max?' She felt herself blush from the toes up.

'Didn't you get my message?' he asked, while she was still trying to get her brain around the fact that he was here, at her door, when her subconscious was telling her that he was in her bed...

'What message?' Then, rubbing her hands over her face in an attempt to wake herself properly, 'No, don't tell me, just come up.' She buzzed him up, blinking the sleep out of her eyes as she checked the time. Eleven-thirty?

She was half an hour short of dream time, but on the other hand she did have the reality.

She yawned, eased her aching limbs, filled the kettle, switched it on. 'I'm in the kitchen,' she said, when she heard the door.

'Ah.'

She turned and was for a moment transfixed.

She couldn't remember the last time she'd seen

Max in anything but a dark suit, or dinner jacket. Wearing a pair of washed-out jeans, an open-neck shirt, soft leather bomber jacket, he looked so much more like the boy she'd once worshipped.

They'd been such friends, had always had such fun until her hormones had got in the way.

She'd missed that so much. Missed him.

Her life, she realised, had never been quite so joyful, quite so sunny, since she'd fallen in lust with him and, too young to hide her feelings, had destroyed something truly special. She ached for that lost innocence. Ached for his friendship...

She swallowed. 'Ah?' she repeated.

He grinned. 'The answer is clearly no. You didn't get my message.'

'Er, no.' She glanced at the answering machine, its red light winking. Frowned as something nudged at her memory.

'Did I get you up?'

'What?' Then, realising how she must look—not so much Saturday casual, as Saturday slob in an old Chinese silk dressing gown hanging open over the baggy T-shirt she favoured for sleepwear, no make-up and her hair standing on end—she belatedly pulled the wrap around her for decency's sake and tied the belt. Ran a hand self-consciously over her hair in an attempt to smooth it down.

'I had a late night,' she said, unhooking a couple

of mugs from the rack. 'It's Saturday, for goodness' sake!'

What she did in her own time was none of his business.

Unlike what she did in her dreams...

'Don't be so defensive, Lou. You've had a long week. How did the launch go last night?'

'Defensive?' Yes, defensive. When had that become her default mode when dealing with Max? She shook her head. 'Sorry. Why don't you just tell me what you said?' she suggested.

'Something along the lines of "Why don't we have lunch at the Chelsea restaurant tomorrow to discuss how we're going to handle the Meridia trip? I know you're busy so don't worry about calling back unless the answer's no..."'

He opened his hands, inviting her response.

Thoughtful, fun...

'Ah,' she said.

'Maybe we could make that brunch? If we have it here you wouldn't have to get dressed.'

Brunch in bed...

No, no, no...

'Um, maybe,' she said, brushing at her cheek as if she could somehow rub away a rerun of the blush. 'I don't know what I've got in. I've been too busy to shop.'

'Eggs?' he suggested, apparently oblivious to her

heightened colour, more interested in the egg basket hanging from the overhead rail. 'Why don't I whip up something while you take your time and wake up?' he suggested, apparently catching on to the fact that she wasn't quite with it.

One of the perks of coming from a family in the restaurant business; everyone had to put in some time in the kitchens and the men didn't think it beneath them to cook.

She found herself smiling. Really smiling. 'That would be nice,' she said. And realised that she meant it.

'Scrambled do you? Coffee?'

'That sounds good,' she said, then, afraid that she was grinning like an idiot, she ducked away, reached for the basket, then yelped as pain shot through her scalp as Max had the same idea.

'Oh, damn! Hold on, your hair is caught in my cuff. Don't move,' he said, unnecessarily, as he lowered his wrist to unravel it, making things worse.

'Don't pull!'

'Sorry. Here…' He lifted his arm, leaned into her, pinning her against the table with the weight of his body as he eased the tension on her hair.

Off balance and held fast, her face pressed into his shoulder, she had no option but to keep still while he tried to work it free, forced to breathe in the scent of leather, freshly laundered linen, something else—nothing that had come from a bottle. Something indefinably male. Memorably Max.

'What's taking you so long?' she mumbled into his shoulder, in danger of drowning in Max-scented air.

'What?' Then, 'Hang on, I've nearly got it...' And then she was free, except that his arm was round her now. And he hadn't moved. 'Okay?' he asked, looking down at her.

Your call, her inner temptress murmured. *Go for it.*

'What?' She shook her head. 'No, I'm very far from okay,' she snapped, pulling free and gasping in sufficient fresh air to wash out the scent of him, rubbing her hands over her arms as if to free herself of the memory of his touch. Then, nursing her tender scalp. 'What kind of idiot are you?'

'The idiot who offered to make you breakfast? As opposed to the idiot with half a yard of hair flapping about in the kitchen.'

'Half a yard of...' Words failed her, but not for long. 'This isn't one of your restaurant kitchens, Max—'

'*Our* restaurant kitchens.'

She'd started off angry with herself, but this miserable attempt to wrong-foot her just made her mad at him.

'This is *my* kitchen, *my* space. I don't have to tie back my hair and put it in a net. When I'm here I don't have to do anything I don't want to.'

For a moment their eyes were locked in a combat of wills, the air crackling between them. Despite all the resolutions she'd made that week to be good, to be *mature*, if she'd had anything to hand other than the egg basket she'd have crowned him with it. Fortunately for him, she knew from experience just how much she hated cleaning up raw egg.

Maybe Max saw her dilemma, remembered the time she'd flung first and thought later, because without warning he began to laugh.

For a moment Louise couldn't decide whether she was outraged or wanted to join him, but while she was thinking about it her mouth took off on its own and a hiccup of laughter escaped before she could slap a hand over her mouth to keep it in.

'Just remember that I'm not some wet-behind-the-ears sous chef you can order around,' she finally managed.

'No?'

Without warning Max was not laughing, but reaching out for her, pulling her close, wrapping his arms around her, enfolding her in his warmth. Not taking his eyes off her as the heat of his athletic body began to seep into her bones.

'No...'

'I won't forget,' he said, mistaking her intuitive denial of her body's response to him for agreement.

Then, his voice soft as velvet tearing, echoed her own thought. 'You have my word…'

'Lou!' The front door slammed shut, making her jump. 'Lou, are you up?'

Cal?

Oh, hell, Cal!

'Time to wake up and smell the sausages, gorgeous!'

She'd known, at the back of her mind, that there was something. If Max had just given her a moment to wake up, properly, five seconds to think straight instead of stunning her brain cells with an overload of pheromones…

It was hard to say who moved first, only that Max was no longer holding her, that somehow she was by the kitchen door, putting as much distance as she could between the two of them before her unwelcome visitor burst in with all the unrestrained enthusiasm of a Labrador pup.

She didn't even know why. They weren't doing anything wrong…

'Damn, Lou,' Cal said, his back to Max as he tossed the keys on the counter, dumped a bag of groceries alongside them without ever taking his eyes off her. 'You looked like sex on a stick last night, but given the choice I'd take you rumpled every time.'

She tried to speak. Make it clear that he would never be given the choice. All that emerged was a croak.

'Shocked into silence by the fact that I've been shopping, eh?' he said, with a grin. 'Needs must,' he said, 'and, let's face it, you didn't have anything in your fridge that a real bloke could eat for breakfast.'

'I wasn't expecting any kind of bloke,' she finally managed, looking anywhere but at Max, knowing what he must be thinking would be written all over his face. And who could blame him? She was the one who'd let him think that she and Cal were more than…than they were. 'Real or otherwise,' she added, helplessly.

'I know, but as always the welcome was as warm as the bed. In fact, my scrumptious, why don't you toddle off back there while I cook you up a CJ special…?'

Max didn't exactly clear his throat. It was more a low growl, alerting Cal to the fact that she was not alone.

He turned, glanced at Max, then at her, and with a careless shrug said, 'Or maybe not.' He turned back to the shopping, began to unpack it. 'No problem. Plenty for three…'

'Thanks for the offer, but I don't do threesomes,' Max replied and, with a nod in her direction, 'You should have told me you had other plans.'

'Max…' she protested. Too late. He wasn't listening. For an answer. An explanation. For anything.

'I'll see you on Monday morning, Louise. Check-in is at six-fifteen. I'll pick you up at five-thirty.' And with that he walked out of the kitchen, without so much as a glance at either of them, closing the front door very quietly behind him as he left.

She remembered that quiet anger.

It was nothing like the flashpoint moments when he'd shouted at her, she'd shouted back; up and down and over in a moment. Well, until that last time, anyway. But that white-lipped quiet when he was too angry to speak, that was something else. She'd seen it when his father's last marriage had broken up, when his brother Jack had given up trying to please their father and walked out of the family home, the business, the country. Losing Jack had been another huge blow for him. The two of them had been so close, but when he'd left Jack had cut himself off from everyone…

Did he think that was happening again? That history was repeating itself with her? Understanding began to filter through the layers of her sleep-fogged brain…

'He seemed a little tense,' Cal said, distracting her.

'He's got a lot on his mind.'

'Oh, right. Just as long as I didn't ruin a special moment.'

She glared at him. Then, because it wasn't his fault, but hers, she said, 'No, Cal. You're all right. Max just wanted to talk about work.'

'On a Saturday?' He grinned. 'Bit keen, isn't he?'

'Keen?' As she laughed she remembered laughing with Max. How good it had felt. 'Describing Max as "keen" about the business is like suggesting Rip van Winkle took a nap.'

'He needs to relax. Take things easy.' Then, 'So… Breakfast?' He reached up and unhooked a frying-pan from the overhead rack.

How ironic that Cal, a man normally so idle that he looked pained if he had to pull the ring on his own beer can, had today of all days decided to do something to justify his keep.

On second thoughts it was far more likely that hunger had driven him to action. That and genuine fear that if he'd woken her, she'd leave him sitting on the pavement next time he turned up unannounced; that he'd have to find a hotel and actually pay for accommodation.

In fact, now she actually looked at him, she realised that his offer of breakfast in bed had been all talk. Far from leaping into action, he was holding the frying-pan in the helpless manner of a man who was making a gesture, assuming that like any sensible woman she'd quickly relieve him of the burden; anything rather than let him loose in her immaculate kitchen.

'Not right now, thanks, Cal,' she said. 'But you go right ahead.'

She ignored his crestfallen expression and instead helped herself from the carton of orange juice he'd so thoughtfully provided. She carried it through to the living room and, in an effort to wipe out the memory of Max's expression as he'd walked out, put one of the *Beach Street* DVDs that Jodie had sent her into the machine. Then she broke open a packet of Tim Tams—if ever a moment called for chocolate—and told herself that she'd go after him later. He'd be easy to find. He'd be in his office, or one of the restaurants. Funnelling his anger, converting it into action, making it work for Bella Lucia.

Not that he had any reason to be angry. She had the sole right to anger in this scenario. How could he think her so shallow, so *easy*?

She'd never bed-hopped. Had discovered the very first time that it was not the way to drive him from her mind. On the contrary. It had only made the longing more desperate. As the chocolate hit her anger began to melt into something dangerously close to regret and, without warning, tears threatened.

'Are you sure I can't fix you a fried-egg sandwich?' Cal called from the kitchen, hopefully. Or was that desperation in his voice?

'I'll pass,' she assured him, then, as the familiar theme tune swept her back to the warmth of

Melbourne, instead of letting go and indulging herself, she found herself wondering why, when Cal was a freeloading pain in the backside without a scruple to his name, she wasn't ever tempted to decorate him with the contents of her egg basket.

Actually, it didn't take a genius to come up with the answer; she wasn't roused to fury by Cal for the simple reason that nothing he did actually mattered to her.

CHAPTER SIX

LOUISE'S attempts to distract herself with *Beach Street* were a dismal failure. Tensed for the sound of the doorbell, waiting for the phone to ring, she was unable to concentrate.

Neither obliged.

Why would they? Max had told her what time he'd pick her up. What else was there to say?

An apology for acting like a jerk, perhaps? Something along the lines of 'It's none of my business who you have staying in your apartment…'

It wasn't any of his business.

Liar!

The little voice that had taken up residence in her head turned up the volume, refusing to be ignored and infuriatingly, she knew that it was right.

The way she'd responded to his kiss, her very bold—

No, she was done with fooling herself; if she was reduced to a blush just thinking about it she'd been a lot more than bold.

The way she'd responded to his kiss, her *brazen* assertion that she considered it no more than a down payment, made it his business.

When Cal had walked into her apartment as if he'd owned it, owned her, Max had had every right to be mad.

Which was the second time she'd been forced to admit, to herself if not to him, that he was right and she was wrong.

Not good.

Okay. Forget the apology, but he'd said he wanted to discuss their trip to Meridia. He might be mad at her, but he still needed to do that. When he'd calmed down he'd call her and she'd be able to tell him that he'd got it totally wrong, that she and Cal were not an item, never had been, never would be, so he could stop behaving like an idiot and get back here.

The thought briefly prompted a smile. Then reality brought her back to earth.

Apart from the fact that Max didn't like anyone telling him he was wrong—which was, of course, what made it such a pleasing proposition—there was the small detail of what would happen next.

Would they pick up where they'd left off? With his arms around her and an expression in his eyes that promised her a world of trouble?

And your problem with that is...?

She swallowed, nervously.

Yes?

'No problem, okay!'

At her outburst, Cal appeared from the kitchen. She glared at him, daring him to comment; he held up his hands in mute surrender and beat a hasty retreat.

No problem, she repeated, but this time silently, in her head. It was time to admit, at least to herself, that she wanted Max to finally lose it, make the kind of passionate, no-holds-barred love to her that he had done in her wicked imagination a thousand times.

Then, surely, she would be able to wipe him from her mind. Get over it. Forget him.

But not right now.

In the past it had always been Max in control of their relationship. Max doing the right thing. Max behaving well...

Just this once she needed to be the one in the driving seat, the one making things happen. If she ran after him, begged him to listen, no matter what happened afterwards, he would still be dictating events.

Abandoning the television, telling herself firmly that whatever he'd wanted to talk about would have to wait until Monday, that she wasn't hanging around the phone waiting for him to climb down off his high horse and get down to work, she went to take a shower. A very cool one. Then she went to her office to finalise the HOTfood account.

Work had always been an escape from her feelings. They had that in common. He'd been right about that, too. He had done her a favour by firing her from the restaurant.

If she hadn't been so angry with Max, so desperate to prove herself, she doubted she'd ever have made such a success of her business. She'd have simply drifted from job to job until she'd settled for marriage, children, domesticity.

She'd come close. But Max was always there. An unfulfilled ache…

She turned on all the lights, reached for the file, and she was doing fine until the cell phone on her desk began to ring.

She made a grab for it, then forced herself to let it ring three times, to take a calming breath, before she looked at the caller ID.

It wasn't Max, but her mother.

The one who'd brought her up. Held her hand when she was nervous. Cuddled her when she was sad. Bathed her knees when she grazed them trying to keep up with Max…

Lied to her.

She wanted to leave it, do what she'd been doing for weeks and let the voicemail pick up, unable to cope with the stilted awkwardness of a conversation where neither of them knew quite what to say, but found she couldn't do it.

'Hello, Mum.'

'Darling? You were so long I thought I was going to get that horrible voicemail thing again.'

'Sorry. I did mean to call you back.'

'I know you're busy.'

'Yes,' she said, hating that her mother felt she had to make excuses for her. 'How are you? How is…?' She closed her eyes, stumbling at the first hurdle, unable to bring herself to say the word. She'd always been Daddy's little girl but the minute he'd discovered he had sons he'd brushed her aside. Second class…

'Good,' her mother said, quickly filling the too obvious silence. 'Daddy's a lot better. Walking the dog, eating plenty of fruit and fish, keeping the stress levels down. Even finding time to play a little golf now he's retired. The heart man is very pleased with him.'

'That's good.'

'Oh, it won't last. He's bored out of his mind, fretting about the business. Whether Max is coping.'

'Coping? You're joking. He's in his element. Full of plans—'

'You've seen him?' Then, not waiting for an answer, as if that too was some information she had no right to, 'I know how capable he is. He shouldn't have had to wait so long for his chance. But Uncle Robert wouldn't retire unless your father did, and you know your father…'

Her mother pulled up again realising, perhaps, that was the one person she didn't know.

'He's fretting, Louise. The restaurant was his life. Maybe if you could come over, go for a walk with him, reassure him…'

No, no…

'That's why I was ringing. Is there any chance of you coming to lunch tomorrow?'

'I don't—'

'No one else, just us,' she said, offering swift reassurance that the prodigal sons wouldn't be there.

How much more painful all this must be for her mother, Louise thought. To have her own inadequacies as a woman so cruelly exposed, to be eclipsed by the sons of a woman who'd taken money from William Valentine to 'disappear'.

'It's been so long since it was just the three of us.'

But it never had been just the three of them. She had another mother and father, John Valentine had sons…

So many lies.

She couldn't… 'I'm just so busy at the moment. I'm in the office now.'

'You work too hard, Louise.'

'I love what I do, but this is different. I'm going to be working for *Bella Lucia* from Monday and I've got a lot to clear up before then.'

'Max managed to persuade you?' Her mother sounded surprised, which was understandable.

given their history. 'Well, that's good news. Daddy will be delighted.'

Her mother's obvious relief that she'd be close, held within the family circle, at least for a while, set up her nerves like a nail on a chalkboard. Was that the real reason why Max wanted her? Not for her talent, but to please her parents? Was that part of the deal he'd made with Jack?

Did it matter? She was in control. She'd do a job that would bring kudos to her own consultancy. Gain an international reputation. It wasn't only Max who could go global.

'We're flying to Meridia at the crack of dawn on Monday,' she said, without comment. Pleasing 'daddy' wasn't any part of *her* plan. 'I'm sorry, but I really will have to give lunch a miss.'

'I understand. Another time. Will you be seeing Emma?' she asked, changing the subject, unwilling to hang up.

'I expect so.'

'Well, give her my love. And make sure you wrap up well. Have you got a really warm coat? The kind of thing you wear in London won't do. It'll be much colder in the mountains.' Then, maybe realising that she was behaving like a fussy mother, she let it go. 'Louise, have you met…?'

This time it was her mother who stumbled, unable to say the word.

'Patsy Simpson?' Lou filled in for her. 'Yes, we had tea together this week.'

You had time for that, that busy little voice whispered in her ear. In the busiest week of your life you still found time for tea with Patsy...

'Oh.'

The sound was small, agonised, as if a knife had just gone in, taking her mother's breath away. Louise knew exactly how she felt. It was the way she'd felt when her father had told her she'd been adopted. Still felt...

'Was it...a success?' Ivy finally managed. 'Will you be seeing her again?'

'We're having dinner next week. I'm meeting her new husband. Max is coming with me...'

Unless he'd changed his mind. Without warning, Louise's throat seized as her eyes filled with tears...

'Louise?'

'I'm sorry, Mum, really, I have to go.'

'Yes, of course. If there's anything...' She caught herself. 'Well, you know.'

Yes. She knew. But it was as if an invisible barrier had been erected between them; where there had been spontaneity, warmth, there was now just this horrible awkward *politeness*.

Her fault.

Ring Ivy. Don't cut yourself off...

Max's words echoed in the empty space where her family had once been. And not just his words. He'd betrayed to her feelings that she'd never suspected, an envy of the warmth of a family life he'd never experienced.

It was for him that she picked up the phone again, rang the familiar number. 'Mum?'

'Louise…'

'I will come. Soon. I promise…'

Max stared at his cell phone, flicking through the names in its memory; the modern equivalent of a little black book. It was Saturday evening and he didn't have a date. Hadn't had a date since before Christmas. Longer. He tried to recall the last time he'd taken a woman out for the evening and discovered that it had been before his grandfather, the patriarchal William Valentine, had died the previous summer, precipitating the events that had thrown the *Bella Lucia* empire into such confusion.

He'd warned Louise that this business was hard on personal lives and he should know. But he was no longer involved in the day to day management of the restaurants. He was now responsible for the entire business and he had to think global, which, conversely, meant that his evenings—should he wish them to be—were suddenly his own.

He glanced again at the phone. There was only

one person he wanted to phone but she was otherwise engaged with her dumb blond Australian, and, giving up, he tossed it onto the chair beside him, staring out unseeing over a Thames that reflected the gun-metal grey of the winter sky.

It was as if his memory had been overwritten and the only face in his brain's database belonged to Louise.

Louise, her blue-grey eyes dancing, hair the colour of a wheat-field in summer, silk beneath his fingertips…

Louise, lips parted as if she were about to say something outrageous…

Louise, eyes more black than grey, lips soft and yielding under his own…

He turned abruptly from the window as the phone began to ring. Picked it up.

Not Louise but his mother.

'Georgie?'

'Max! Darling! How are you?'

'Fine.' He fought down the surge of feelings, of hope that for once she was calling him just for a chat. Like a real mother. 'You?' he asked.

'Well, actually, darling, I'm in a little bit of bother…'

Left with the choice of calling Max and putting him straight, spending what was left of the afternoon working, or going home and playing handmaid to her unwanted guest, Louise decided on none of the above and went shopping, instead.

She found a beautiful coat in a bright, cheering red cashmere that came nearly to her ankles. Utterly gorgeous and warm enough to please a dozen mothers, she told herself as she opened her bag to take out her wallet. Then discovered that she was holding her cell phone.

Call him...

She shook her head, fighting off the memory of that moment in the kitchen when Max had held her, looked at her as if the only thing he'd wanted was to make her dream a reality. Before she could do anything she'd regret, she pushed her phone to the bottom of her bag out of harm's way, found her wallet and paid for her coat.

Then she went in search of a hat, boots—no point in doing half a job—and threw in a scarf and lined gloves for good measure.

Then she undid all that good work by splurging on some gossamer silk underwear that had a tog value on the minus side of the scale.

Her subconscious did no more than raise its eloquent eyebrows. They said, 'So, who did you buy those for?'

She ignored it.

Thermal underwear was taking sensible too far.

Cal did his best to interest her in going clubbing that evening, but she pleaded pressure of work. Instead she phoned Jodie, spending an hour telling her about meeting their mother and catching up with her news, then made a cup of cocoa, and, determined on a early night, went to bed with nothing for company but a couple of books she'd found about Meridia.

She hadn't been to the gym all week and after yet another dream-filled night—this time spent chasing something unnamed, unseen that she was glad to wake from—she went and worked up a good sweat before going home and finishing off the Tim Tams for breakfast.

After that she spent the rest of the day at her office with her cell phone switched off and by the time she got home Cal had gone, leaving the flat a tip. Presumably the wilting flowers were his idea of thanks for her hospitality. She tossed them in the bin and got out the vacuum cleaner, glad to have something to keep her occupied. Stop her from dwelling on the fact that none of the messages on her machine had been from Max.

When the doorbell rang on the dot of five-thirty on Monday morning, Louise flipped the switch and said, 'I'll be right down.'

She slipped into her new coat, set the black velvet

beret at a jaunty angle on her head, picked up her roomy shoulder bag and went downstairs.

Max was waiting in the car with the engine running.

'Got everything?' he asked as she slid in beside him, clipped her seat belt into place.

So much for Miss Business Efficiency of whatever year you cared to mention.

What was the point when she didn't even get a 'good morning'?

'Everything important,' she replied and ticking them off on her fingers, 'Hairspray, lipstick, emergency nail repair kit...' She looked across at him, suddenly wanting not to make him angry, but to make him laugh. 'Safety pins...'

If he was tempted to smile, he did a manful job of hiding it and, too late to do any good, she wished she'd kept a rein on her temper, or at least her tongue.

A first, that.

They made the airport in what must have been some kind of record, for silence as well as speed, on roads that were relatively clear so early in the morning. Although half an hour had never felt so long.

Things didn't improve when they reached the terminal building. Max just leaned across her, took an envelope out of the glove compartment and handed it to her.

'You handle the check-in while I go and park.'

Unmistakably an order and considering it was combined with the silent treatment her immediate reaction was to tell him to stuff Meridia, stuff Bella Lucia and to go run his own errands. But even as she opened her mouth she found herself recalling her earlier regret and—another first—kept her peace.

'Right. Well, I'll be—'

'I'll find you, Louise,' he said, cutting her short. Then, 'Will you please move, before I get a parking ticket?'

She manfully resisted the temptation to drop his passport and the tickets in the nearest bin and take a taxi home, but he was unappreciative of her restraint and once they were boarded, closed his eyes, suggesting that even silence was a strain. That he couldn't bear to look at her.

Because he thought that she was involved with Cal? Nothing else had changed since the evening they'd spent talking about the business over supper, not touching, keeping their distance after that searing kiss.

Which meant what, exactly?

That he was jealous?

She glanced at him as if some clue might be found in his posture. In the give-away tension around his closed eyes as she watched him.

'Are you together?' The stewardess, breakfast tray

in hand, joined her in regarding Max, unsure whether or not to disturb him.

'Never met him before in my life,' Louise replied, turning away and smiling up at the woman.

'Oh. Right. I don't suppose he said anything about breakfast, then?' The woman sounded harassed. No doubt someone had already given her a hard time for trying to do her job, something Max would never do. He knew the stresses and was always considerate of anyone in the service industry.

Unless it was her, of course.

He'd always made an exception in her case.

And recalling her revelatory thoughts about Cal, she asked herself, So why would he bother? Unless he cared?

The stewardess was still waiting.

'Breakfast? Oh, wait, he did say something about looking forward to it.' Feeling a desperate urge to smile, she instead raised her eyebrows, inviting the woman to agree that he was clearly crazy. 'I guess he didn't have time to eat before he left for the airport.'

That finally did raise a smile—or maybe it was a grimace—and Max opened his eyes, straightened in his seat.

'Now would be a very good time to use one of those safety pins, Louise,' he said. 'To fasten your lips together.'

Max regretted the words the minute they left his

mouth. He'd spent most of the weekend reminding himself that it was always a mistake to mix business with pleasure, but when she'd swept out of the front door in that dramatic scarlet coat, sexy little hat, common sense had taken a hike. Even so, he'd thought he'd covered himself with the most innocuous of remarks.

"*Got everything?*" What was there to take offence at in that?

And now he'd done it again. This time with intent.

Apparently they couldn't be together for more than a minute without one of them lighting the blue touchpaper. This time he was the guilty party and there was an apparently endless moment while he waited for the explosion. He was ready for it, wanted it, he realised in a moment of searing self-revelation. At least when they were fighting he knew he had her total attention. That she wasn't thinking about anyone but him.

It didn't happen.

Instead of taking the tray from the still hovering stewardess and tipping it in his lap, she leaned forward, picked up her bag and, from a miniature sewing kit, extracted a clip of tiny gold safety pins.

She unhooked one, turned and offered it to him. 'Go ahead, Max.'

In the clear bright light of thirty thousand feet, her eyes were a pure translucent silver and for a moment he couldn't think, speak, move.

'Whenever you're ready,' she prompted. And pushed out her lips, inviting him to get on with it.

It was all he could do to stop the brief expletive slipping from his own lips.

'It's a bit small,' was the best he could manage. 'The pin,' he added, quickly, in case she thought he was referring to her mouth.

Too late, he realised that there was no safe answer as she lifted one brow and said, 'So, I have a big mouth.'

Pushing him, inviting him to do his worst…

He felt a surge of relief. This was better. 'Too big for this pin,' he said, closing his hand around hers. Happy to oblige.

They were six miles above the earth. Where could she go?

'Sorry about that,' she said.

Her mouth was innocent of a smile but without warning a dimple appeared in her left cheek and he felt a surge of warmth, knowing—because he knew her as no one else did—that it was there.

'I'm rarely called to pin up anything bigger than a shoestring strap, or a broken zip at a photo-shoot.' The dimple deepened as if she were having serious trouble keeping the smile at bay. 'I'll make a note to pack something larger in future.'

'Good plan,' he said, taking the pin, letting go of her hand. Touching her was firing up the kind of heat that no shower was cold enough to suppress. 'In the meantime I'll hang onto this one, just in case.'

'In case of what?'

'Just "in case"', he said, dropping it into his ticket pocket. 'Who knows when one will encounter a shoestring-strapped damsel in distress?'

Then, because this elegant, perfectly groomed version of Louise was so different from the way she'd looked on Saturday, warm, tousled and sleepy from the bed she'd shared with Cal Jameson—when for a moment he'd looked into her eyes and seen himself reflected there, as if he were the centre of her soul—he turned away, unable to bear it.

'I'll pass on the food, thanks,' he said to the stewardess. 'Just leave me the juice.'

'Me, too,' Louise said. Then, turning to him, 'Do you want to run through what we're doing today, Max?'

Not as much as he'd hoped, but work had always served him well enough in the past.

'Why not?' And he watched as she produced a folder, opened it, handed him a copy of the papers. Within minutes he was absorbed in the ideas she'd managed to throw together over the weekend. 'Impressive,' he said. 'Considering the distractions.'

For some reason that made her smile.

'I spoke to my mother, too. Ivy…'

'You called her?'

'She called me. She wanted me to go to lunch yesterday.'

'Perhaps there was something in the stars.' She frowned, not understanding. 'My mother called me, as well. She wanted me to bail her out of jail.'

He hadn't meant to tell her. He'd never told anyone. Not his father, not Jack. She was his mother. His cross.

'Max…' Louise laid her hand over his. 'I'm so sorry. Is she in desperate trouble?'

'Nothing that money won't sort out. Unpaid bills. It just took a bit of sorting out.'

'I would have helped.'

'I didn't need any help,' he said. He didn't need anyone. 'I've done it all before.'

'It's a shame we didn't make it to the fishing lodge,' Louise said as they returned to the chauffeur-driven car Sebastian had thoughtfully laid on for them.

The day had just ebbed away. Lunch with Emma and Sebastian had been unexpected. Wonderful, but even an informal, private lunch with the king and his new queen was not exactly an eat-and-run deal. Then the meeting with a leading hotelier had been long on formality, short on substance, and who could know that the Director of Tourism thought he had to 'sell' them Meridia? Organise a tour of the city, with stops at all the historic sites. It would have been unpardonably rude to tell him they were already 'sold', but it had left them too short of time to get out to the island in daylight.

Now they barely had time to make their check-in at the airport and, although Max had said nothing, it was as clear as day what he was thinking. That the wasted time was entirely down to her.

'I should have listened to you, Max, instead of trying to cram everything in. We're going to have to make another trip to look at it.'

'That won't be necessary.'

She stopped, stared after him. He'd didn't even want to look? Was rejecting it sight unseen. Had he just been stringing her along, making some crappy pay back point about leaping before they'd looked…?

'You've decided against it?' she demanded, already regretting jumping in to take the blame.

Realising that she wasn't keeping pace with him, he turned to face her.

'No, Louise. On the contrary. I want to see it very much, but I thought it likely that we'd need more time so I've arranged for us to stay over until tomorrow.'

'Oh.' She should have felt happy that he was, after all, enthusiastic about the project, but instead she felt oddly flattened. Excluded. Was that how he'd felt when she'd gone ahead and made arrangements without talking to him first? 'You didn't think to mention it?' she asked as she joined him and they moved on.

'I did, but at the time you were otherwise occupied.' It was true—Emma had claimed her attention over lunch, wanting to talk about the coming ball. Ask her advice... 'Is it a problem?' Max asked, standing back so that she could step into the rear of the car, then joining her. 'We could always stop somewhere to buy a toothbrush.'

'Not necessary.'

She glanced at him, then quickly looked away.

They'd been sitting shoulder-to-shoulder close for most of the day, but clearly regretting letting slip his problems with his mother—showing a chink in his armour—he'd kept his distance mentally, put up some kind of invisible wall between them. Maybe it had simply been a business thing, a protection against the simmering undercurrent that was always there, just beneath the surface.

Now they were on their own for the first time since they'd landed, she was doubly conscious of his nearness, not as a business colleague, but as a man.

'I never travel without one,' she said, aware that he had looked at her, querying her response. 'A toothbrush.' The 'everything' she hadn't got around to listing for him was her emergency pack consisting of spare underwear, a clean T-shirt and a toothbrush; having been held up by delays on more than one occasion, she never travelled without it.

'Nor do I.' Then, 'I'm sorry if I've interfered with your plans for the evening. Did you have something special arranged?'

'On a Monday? After a full day travelling? Are you crazy?' Then realising what he meant, she added, coolly, provocatively, 'Just an early night.' And felt a curious mixture of feelings as his jaw tightened. A giddy heart lift that he cared enough to feel jealousy at the thought of Cal Jameson in her bed. Regret that, despite the changes in their relationship, the fact that he'd felt able to open up a little to her about his own problems—and whoever would have believed Max Valentine had problems?—they were both still caught up in a loop, unable to break the habit of striking first, thinking later. 'So?' she prompted. 'Where are we staying?'

'At the lodge,' he replied, equally cool. Equally provocative. 'We'll have all night to make ourselves familiar with the interior, consider the possibilities and, if we're still interested, all day tomorrow to look around the island.' He paused briefly. 'I trust the arrangements I've made meet with your approval.'

She frowned. Did he really think she'd object? Or was it that he was still so angry with her that he felt he had to score points?

After the incident with the safety pin they'd both been on their best behaviour, managing an entire day without rubbing each other up the wrong way. Now, with no one around to see, they were, apparently, to return to sniping terms.

Well, not her. Not any more. 'They do, Max,' she said, very quietly. 'I should have thought of it myself.'

'You've been fully occupied with your own affairs, no doubt.'

'It has been quite a week,' she agreed, even though she was certain he wasn't referring to the HOTfood re-launch, but holding to her determination not to be roused. 'Twelve-hour days as standard. But as of five-thirty this morning, I'm all yours.'

'I think not.'

It was probably fortunate that the car pulled alongside the jetty at that moment, that they were fully occupied transferring themselves to a launch that was waiting to ferry them across to the island. It was hard work being this good when she wasn't getting any help.

But the journey gave them a fairy-tale view of the city from the lake, the floodlit ancient castle, layer upon layer of lights descending and then reflected back in the ripples. They stood in the bows and watched its retreat before turning to each other.

'That's a good start,' Max said.

'Magical. I'm glad we had a chance to see it at

night.' Then as the boat slowed she turned to see the approach to the island, the fishing lodge. Equally magical. 'Come on, let's see if the arrival lives up to the journey.'

It did. A liveried footman was waiting at the jetty to lead them up a broad flight of stone steps that opened out onto a wide terrace, through a pair of huge, two-storey height doors. Once inside a vast entrance hall, the footman bowed them into the hands of a butler, before disappearing.

'Good evening, Sir. Madam.' He took their coats, passing them on to a hovering maid, and already Louise's mind was working overtime.

They could keep all this, she thought. Sell it as a chance to be treated like royalty…

'I'll show you to your room,' he said, leading the way up a wide wooden staircase that opened up onto a magnificent first-floor gallery with rooms on three sides. The lodge might have been small by castle standards, but not by any other measure.

He opened a door, crossed the room. 'Your dressing room and bathroom are here, Madam.' Then, turning to Max, 'What time do you wish dinner to be served, sir?'

'Not too late. It's been a long day,' Max said. 'Seven-thirty?'

'Certainly. A fire has been lit in the drawing room. Please ring and ask for anything you want.'

And with that the man was gone, leaving them both in a vast room dominated by an ornately draped and very high four-poster bed. At its foot, on a low chest, stood their bags.

Side by side.

CHAPTER SEVEN

THERE was a long moment of silence, then Louise cleared her throat and said, 'I think there must have been a slight misunderstanding. The butler must have assumed we were husband and wife, rather than...

She stopped. It was hard to break the habit of a lifetime. Max was not family. And sharing a room with him, a bed with him, was her darkest dream...

'I'll go and sort it out,' he said.

'No.' The word escaped her before she could corral it, keep it safely locked up.

Maybe.

Maybe she didn't try as hard as she might have done.

This felt like fate saying, '*Now...*'

'No?' he repeated, his face expressionless, giving nothing away. For a moment, when he'd taken the pin from her, kept it, anything had seemed possible. Since then he'd kept all interaction on a strictly business level, kept his distance, not just physically, but emotionally.

'I'm desperate for a cup of tea,' she said, losing her nerve. 'Let me freshen up and then we can both go.'

'I thought you might want a little privacy in order to phone your Antipodean friend,' he said, stiffly. 'Explain that you won't be home tonight.'

'I don't have to explain myself to anyone, Max, least of all Cal Jameson.' Or him, for that matter, but it was time to put an end to this. Set the record straight. 'And after the state he and some girl he brought home with him on Saturday night left my flat in, he's very far from being my friend. In fact the next time I find him on my doorstep at two in the morning, I'll be very tempted to leave him there.'

'Girl?' Max repeated, homing in on the one important word, going to the heart of what she was telling him.

'He must have picked her up when he went clubbing. They woke me coming in at some unearthly hour…' Then, all innocence, 'Oh, please. You didn't think *I* was sleeping with him, did you?'

'You implied as much—'

'No, Max,' she said cutting him off, dropping the pretence. 'You implied it. In front of a valued client, what's more. *You* implied I was sleeping with him, too, I seem to recall, which might have been funny if it hadn't been so insulting.'

'*He* certainly implied as much.'

'Cal? Or Oliver Nash?'

His mouth tightened. 'You know who I mean.'

'Well, yes. Apart from the fact that he's married, Oliver is far too much a gentleman to have done anything of the sort.'

'Not too married, or too much of a gentleman, to be above asking you out to dinner.'

'Too much of a gentleman to have boosted his ego by implying I was sleeping with him.' Then, furious with him for being so dense. 'The man's an incorrigible flirt, Max, but it doesn't mean anything.'

'It might have meant nothing to you, but I can assure you that given half an inch of encouragement, he'd have been in like Flynn.'

Jealous, jealous, her heart sang…

'He didn't have any encouragement because I never mix business with pleasure,' she said, firmly. 'As for Cal, he's like a big overgrown puppy. He understands the word no, but believes that if he ignores it, I'll forget I said it.' Then, because it was suddenly vital that he was absolutely clear. 'The most intimate exchange between us was that kiss under the mistletoe at the family party. In full view of everyone.'

'But you went home with him.'

'Yes, well…' She turned away, feeling hideously exposed, but knowing that she had to clear the air between them if they were going to work together.

If they were ever going to finish what they'd started. 'Taking Cal home wasn't my idea of fun, but Jodie found the idea of sharing her honeymoon with her brother-in-law less than enthralling and, since she'd sent him gift-wrapped as my date for the evening, I returned the favour by letting him stay in my spare room.' She looked back at him, willing him to understand, cut her some slack. 'It's what sisters do, Max. They help each other out. You'd have done the same for Jack, wouldn't you?'

'Taken home a good-looking woman who fancied the pants off me to give Jack some space with Maddie? I could see how that might work,' he said.

'Oh, forget it!' She grabbed her bag, headed for the bathroom.

'No.' He raked long fingers through his hair, ruffling it in a way that she found unbearably sexy. 'I'm sorry. Tell me.'

An apology from Max now? They were coming along…

'There's nothing to tell, Max. That's the point. Except that Cal now treats my flat like his own personal hotel, turning up unannounced whenever he's passing through.'

'I'm sorry, Lou.' Another apology? 'I should have called you, offered to take you to the Christmas party.'

No, this wasn't an apology. It was something far more significant…

Afraid he'd see, read the unbearable yearning in her eyes, she turned quickly away with, 'Oh, right. Like I'd have said yes.'

She didn't wait for his response, but scooted into the bathroom, not coming out until she'd combed her hair, freshened her lipstick. Wiped the need from her face.

'I'll see you downstairs,' she said, when she emerged, heading for the door before he could say any more. Not looking at him, because to look at him was—as it had always been—to invite disaster.

She rang the bell, explained about the rooms, asked for tea, and by the time Max joined her the footman had returned with a tray laden with tea things, accompanied by a maid with a three-tiered tray containing tiny sandwiches, cakes, pastries.

'You know, I don't think we need a hotelier,' Louise said as she handed Max a cup of tea. 'I think we just need to keep these people on to run the place.'

'I doubt they'd want to trade the quiet life they have at present for the long hours and hard work of the commercial world.'

'I was…' Joking. 'Never mind.' She shook her head, putting down her own cup. 'I'm going to take a look around.'

Without waiting for him, she walked out into the magnificent entrance hall with its marble tiled floor, grand staircase, open hearth in which a fire had been lit since their arrival.

'This would make a perfect wedding venue,' Max said, joining her. Then, taking the lead, opening the door to a richly decorated banqueting room, 'It's not quite the way I imagined it would be.'

'You pictured stone walls running with damp, cold enough to freeze your marrow?'

'No, but a fishing lodge does suggest a certain rustic finish.'

'Yes, well, maybe we were being a little too literal in our use of the word. According to Emma, "going fishing" turns out to have been something of a euphemism within the royal family for meeting the mistress. This place might look mediaeval, but it was actually built as a *folie d'amour* by some goaty minor royal in the late nineteenth century. It's practically new by Meridian standards.'

'You weren't just discussing ball dresses when you disappeared for girl talk, then?'

She gave him a withering look. 'It belongs to a branch of the family who spent money like water and lived a hedonistic lifestyle. The owner of this place is what used to be known as a "remittance man". He's paid a pension by the old king to stay away. Sebastian takes care of the running costs, pays the staff just to keep them in work. Nothing would please him more than to see it put to good use.' Then, as if as an afterthought, 'He is also extremely keen to expand the tourist industry.'

'I know.'

'You do?'

'We discussed all this at length when he rang me last week.'

'He rang you?'

'He wanted me to know, if I was serious, that local laws mean I would have to have a Meridian partner, which isn't a problem. As you already pointed out, we'll need someone to run the residential side of the property.' He looked around. 'He also wanted me to know that it will have to be preserved as it is.'

'And no doubt Bella Lucia will be responsible for conserving it?'

'That would be the deal.' He looked up at the gilded ceiling. 'It's a good one, too. We couldn't hope to find anything like this; certainly couldn't build it.' Then, 'The only thing he didn't tell me was how beautiful it is.'

'Maybe he thought you knew.' She gazed about her. 'So, was that one of the things you planned to discuss with me on Saturday?'

He smiled. 'You'll never know, will you? Shall we continue the tour?'

They found a library, a billiard room with a

number of rather splendid stuffed fish mounted in glass cases—possibly the origin of the 'fishing' euphemism—a charming morning room and a vast, heated conservatory.

'Oh, yes,' Max said, turning slowly to take it all in.

'You like it?' Louise asked, only then realising just how important it was to her to have got it right. Demonstrated her worth.

'This would make a perfect informal restaurant, spilling out onto the terrace in summer. We'd have the formal dining room for weddings, functions, parties and there are a couple of smaller rooms for other private parties.'

'It would suit those small, high-level business conferences, too,' she pointed out. 'There are what? Ten, twelve bedrooms? A honeymoon suite for bridal parties…'

'It has everything. And it will be completely different from all our other restaurants, too. Meridia's Bella Lucia will be unique, total luxury.'

'You already have a name for it?'

'It names itself. And about the staff, I was wondering if they'd be prepared to stay on and train the new people?'

She smiled. 'We could ask them.'

He nodded. 'Maybe you'd like to talk to them tomorrow. While I'm inspecting the kitchens, cellar and the utilities. The public rooms will need very little work. I don't think we'll find anywhere else that we can take over so easily.' He turned, touched her arm. 'It's a great start. Thank you, Louise.'

'You're welcome,' she said, tucking a loose strand of hair behind her ear. Looking at the ceiling, desperate not to show him how pleased she was.

He didn't let go, didn't stop looking at her.

'Louise…'

She waited, certain he was going to say something important, not about business, but about them. But after a moment he shook his head, let her go.

'I'd better take a shower before dinner,' she said, needing to escape, catch her breath. 'I'll see you down here just before seven-thirty.'

She managed to walk from the room, but then bolted up the stairs, shutting the door behind her and leaning against it. Afraid he'd follow her. Afraid he wouldn't…

The maid who was waiting for her kept her face carefully expressionless as she said, 'Shall I draw you a bath, Miss Valentine?'

She took a breath, pulled herself together. A shower. She should take a cold shower…

She shivered at the thought. Rejected it.

'Thank you…?'

'Maria, miss.'

'Thank you, Maria. That would be wonderful.'

'Since you don't have any luggage, miss, Her

Royal Highness said you might like to choose a dress from the wardrobe.'

The girl opened up a huge walk-in closet lined with racks of dresses, shoes and everything that went with them.

'Oh, my goodness…' She walked along the racks looking at the elegant vintage gowns, touching the delicate fabrics. Black, beaded silk, sapphire lace, slipper silk in all colours… 'These are beautiful. Who owned them?'

The maid shrugged. 'I've no idea, miss. The count used to have parties here. In the old days.'

Louise picked out an art deco sliver of pearl-grey silk, held it against her.

'They shouldn't be here. They should be in a museum.' Then, 'No…' She'd seen gowns in museums. Dead things. Bits of cloth that looked nothing without a living, breathing person inside them.

'Yes, miss?' Louise shook her head. 'I'll run your bath.'

'Thank you,' she said, then picked up the phone, called Emma.

'Hi, Lou! What do you think of our little castle?'

'It's absolutely beautiful, Emma, perfect, but, tell me, did you know there are dozens of fabulous vintage gowns, shoes, everything here?'

'The mistress's wardrobe? I've heard about it.'

'My dear, you should see it! Have you any idea just how hot vintage clothes are right now? You were looking for something special for your ball—well, I think this could be it. A fashion show—I'm sure you could round up some celebrities for that. Then they could be auctioned off—it's been done before. The press will be salivating, it will bring in all the Hollywood divas and your charity will raise a mint…'

'Louise! You are a genius. I don't suppose I could talk you into organising it for me?'

'Oh, please! Try and stop me!'

'There's just one condition.'

'Anything.'

'You'll be doing this for charity so you won't get a fee, but I want you to have something.'

'No, I'll do it for…' for the family, that was what she'd been going to say '…for you.'

'You've already done so much for me, Lou. Now it's my turn to repay the favour. My condition is that you wear one of those dresses tonight.'

'But… But suppose I spill red wine down it?'

'Drink white if it worries you, but that's the deal.'

'You know, Emma, since you got to be Queen, you have become *so* bossy!' She smiled. 'Thank you.'

Max, having been shown, with profound apologies for an error that had been no one's fault but his own, to another room, found a footman laying out a slightly old-fashioned dinner jacket and dress shirt. His initial response was to say thanks, but no, thanks, but it occurred to him that they would have found something for Louise, too, and she wouldn't hurt their feelings by rejecting it.

He was the only one she didn't care about hurting. Telling him one thing with her eyes, another with everything she did, said. If she ever found out the truth…

He went downstairs at seven-fifteen so that she wouldn't be left on her own, took the whisky the butler poured for him, but, too restless to sit in the drawing room, he paced the hall, his head full of the new restaurant, which of a number of world-class chefs he might tempt to take charge of the kitchen, the start-up costs…

All it took to distract him was a whisper of silk and he turned, looked up.

Louise, her hair twisted up and held in place with some kind of exotic jewelled clip, her hand trailing lightly on the banister rail, draped in a slender silk gown whose soft folds displayed every curve of her body, clung to her long thighs as she moved, was slowly descending the stairs.

For a moment he was transfixed.

He'd seen her dressed for an occasion countless times before; looking like a queen for some other man. But this time she'd dressed for no one but him…

Regaining the use of his limbs, he crossed to meet her and instead of the usual sarcastic remark—gauged to provoke a response guaranteed to leave them both despising the other—he said the first thing that came into his mind.

'You look absolutely stunning, Louise.'

'Thank you,' she said as she reached the bottom step. 'I didn't intend my entrance to be quite such a Hollywood performance, but the dress is a little long and the footwear...' she hitched up her skirt an inch or two to display a matching high-heeled sandal '...is a little on the large side. The stairs required extreme care.'

'I enjoyed every moment of it,' he assured her, then as a clock began to chime the half-hour the butler appeared to announce that dinner was served.

Max extended his arm. 'May I escort you in to dinner, Miss Valentine?'

She smiled, laid her arm along his. 'Thank you, Mr Valentine.'

Dinner was served to them in a small dining room that they had missed on their exploration. Richly decorated on the most intimate scale.

It was a room plainly made for lovers, yet despite their surroundings, the wonderful food, fine wines, exquisite clothes, he felt himself retreat a little, become more distant, determined to keep the conversation firmly fixed on the safe subject of business. He laid out his ideas, she offered marketing, PR strategies.

Neither of them wanted coffee, and when they moved to the drawing room so that the staff could clear away Louise didn't settle, refused a nightcap. His overwhelming reaction was relief. The entire day had been a strain and he needed to escape from this brittle concord before he did, or said, something to shatter it.

'I'm ready for bed, Max.'

'It's been a long day. We'll take it easy tomorrow, just potter around. Take a load of photographs. Come on, I'll see you to your room.'

'I'm not helpless,' she said as he took her arm, shivering a little at the unexpected contact.

'Not helpless, but at the mercy of those shoes. I'm not prepared to risk my most valuable asset taking a tumble and breaking her neck.'

She glanced at him, as if surprised, although why she would be when he'd made it plain that he'd do anything to get her to join him, but she said nothing until they reached her door.

Instead of opening it, ducking quickly inside, as he'd expected her to, she turned to face him, said, 'You never did tell me what you wanted to talk to me about on Saturday, Max.'

'To be honest I was rather hoping we could both forget Saturday.'

'All of it?'

Not the moment when he'd seen her standing in her kitchen, hair tousled, flushed from bed. Her wrap hanging open, her lovely legs bare. Not the moment when she'd looked up at him as if he were the only man she'd ever wanted…

'Maybe just the last bit, where I behaved like a moron.'

'I don't want to forget that part, Max,' she said, her voice so soft that he had to bend his head to catch the words. 'You wouldn't have reacted that way if…'

She hesitated as if to say the words would be to expose them both so he said them for her.

'If I hadn't wanted to throttle Cal Jameson. If I hadn't wanted you for myself.'

Now…

The voice in Louise's head was so loud that she was certain Max must hear it too. But he didn't move.

'This room,' she managed. 'It wasn't a mistake, was it?'

Max shook his head and, emboldened by a tiny sigh that escaped her, said, 'It wasn't a spur-of-the-moment decision. I realised we'd need more time and when I spoke to Sebastian, I asked if we could stay here. He gave me the number so that I could make my own arrangements with the staff; the butler misunderstood and I didn't correct his mistake. I thought, hoped that this might be somewhere private, neutral ground where we could continue our discussion about exactly where you wanted me to kiss you.' He looked up, met her gaze head-on. 'A place where we could conclude all contractual obligations to your complete satisfaction.'

She came close to smiling. 'In an icy, rustic stone lodge?'

'You wouldn't have felt the cold,' he assured her.

'No?'

She shivered, despite the heating, but still he didn't touch her, even though her body was doing everything but scream at him to go for it, even though she could feel that his hand, still supporting her elbow, was not quite steady...

He was giving her total control. Her call...

She opened the bedroom door and led him inside, turning to face him as the door closed behind them

'Show me,' she said, her voice scarcely strong enough to reach him and, lifting her hand, she touched a fingertip to her cheek. 'Kiss me here.'

His eyes seemed to take on a new intensity and for a moment she was afraid that she'd unleashed a passion that he wouldn't be able to hold in check but when, after a pause that seemed to last a lifetime, his lips touched her cheek she felt no more than a whisper of warmth. Enough to send a flash of heat through her and for a moment she swayed towards him, dangerously close to flinging herself on him. If he made one move…

But he didn't. He was leaving her to set the pace, take it where she dared.

If she had the courage.

Responding to his unspoken challenge, she moved her hand, touched her chin.

'Here,' she said, on a breath.

His eyes, darker than pitch, warned her that she was playing a dangerous game. Did he think she didn't know that?

This was their time. Now. It would be brief, glorious but brief, like a New Year's Eve rocket, and afterwards, when it had burnt out, she would be free of him.

They would both be free…

'Here,' she said, raising the stakes, touching her lower lip, anticipating the same exhilarating, no-holds-barred kiss with which he'd stopped her walking away. Would use this time to carry them both over the threshold of restraint and beyond thought.

But he did no more than touch her lower lip, tasting it with his tongue. It was all she could do to remain on her feet; her only compensation was knowing how hard this must be for him. To hold back, wait. It would have been difficult to say which of them was trembling more, but he was forcing her to make all the moves, insisting that she be the one to tip it over the edge from a teasing game into a dark and passionate reality.

'Now, Max,' she said. Unfastening her dress, she let it fall in a shimmering puddle of silk at her feet, leaving her naked but for the scrap of silk and lace at her hips, lace-topped hold-ups, high-heeled sandals.

His response was to pull loose his tie, remove his jacket and toss it aside, finally turning the key in the lock without ever taking his eyes off her.

She'd thought she'd die with the sheer force of desire his first kiss brought bubbling to the surface, but now every cell in her body seemed to sigh, melt as his mouth kissed a slow seductive trail over her breasts and down across the soft curve of her stomach.

In that moment she felt like a conqueror, a queen receiving tribute from a vanquished king whom she'd made her slave.

But then he hooked his thumbs under the ties of her silk panties removing the last barrier between them, using his mouth until 'now' became not a command, not permission to touch, but a whimper-ing entreaty, a plea for his hands, his body, for all he had to give, and she knew that she'd made a mistake.

As he finally took pity on her, responded to her 'Max…please…', lifting her acquiesent body in his arms, carrying her to the great four-poster, she discovered that, far from being the one in control, she was the conquered.

Louise woke in a series of gentle waves. First there was a boneless, almost out-of-body consciousness in which she was dimly aware that it was morning, but felt no pressure to do anything about it. Then came a gradual awareness of a soft pillow beneath her cheek, limbs heavy with the delicious languor of utter contentment.

She nestled down into the pillow, unwilling to relinquish her dreams.

Something warm tickled her shoulder.

She twitched away, burrowed deeper.

It happened again and this time she reached to pull up the sheet, tuck it in, but instead of the sheet her hand encountered warm skin over hard bone.

Her face still buried in the pillow, she flattened her hand over a nose that wasn't quite straight, a mouth blowing soft, warm breath against her palm.

Not a dream, she thought, as finally awake she recalled where she was, who she was with. Every word, every touch, every little whimper as she begged him to love her. Every fierce sound she'd wrung from him in return…

She turned her head, opened her eyes.

Propped on an elbow, he'd clearly been watching her, waiting for her to wake. The fact that he'd grown impatient sent a ripple of delight coursing through her veins and she slid her fingers through his hair, fantasy fulfilled; she had never seen his short, thick, perfectly groomed hair without wanting to do that. Disturb the outer perfection, shatter his control. She'd done that, she thought, in a moment that was pure victory. Then she rolled over onto her back, drawing him to her.

She'd wanted to be free of him, of the dark primal need for him that had destroyed every other relationship. But there was no hurry. She had until the fourteenth to put together her PR and marketing plan. All the time in the world.

'Did anyone ever tell you, Max,' she said, 'that when you wake a woman from her dreams, you have to replace them with something more…substantial?'

'First you have to tell me your dreams, my sweet,' he said, his smile slow and lazy, his eyes smoky-soft in the early-morning light. 'Tell me all your dreams, your wildest fantasies, and I promise you that I'll do whatever it takes to make them come true.'

'You promise?' The word sent a tiny shiver of apprehension sweeping through her. She dismissed it, said, 'Have we got that long?'

CHAPTER EIGHT

'WELL, that's a give-away smile. Who is he?'

Louise, lost in her thoughts, hadn't realised she was smiling and abruptly straightened her face. 'He?'

'Oh, come on.' Gemma, her PA, was grinning fit to bust herself. 'Only a nomination for an award, or a new man in your life, could put a smile that wide on your face. Since it isn't the award season…' She held out her hands, palms up, in a gesture that said 'case proved'. 'So, come on. Give.' Then, slapping her forehead, 'No, don't tell me—'

'If you insist,' Louise replied, more than willing to change the subject. 'Did Max send over the artist's impressions of the Qu'Arim restaurant? He said he'd have them here by lunchtime.'

Was her voice quite steady as she said his name? Should saying 'Max' be quite such a secret pleasure when she was supposed to be clearing him from her system?

'You've used your royal connections to hook yourself a Meridian prince,' Gemma continued as if she hadn't been interrupted. '*That's* the reason you stayed over for an extra day.'

'Just call me Princess Louise,' she agreed. 'The drawings?'

'Hmm, not a prince. You didn't blush.'

'I'm a PR consultant, Gem. I do not blush.'

'If you say so.' Then, 'You can't have any secrets from your PA, Lou. It's not allowed. If I don't know what you're up to,' she said, sitting down and propping her elbows on the desk, 'I won't be able to fend off questions from the press when they get wind of it.'

'Don't worry about it. In the unlikely event that the press should show any interest in who I'm dating you have my full permission to tell them everything you know.'

'Unlikely? Are you kidding? You dropped off the gossip planet when you split with James. As far as the diary hacks are concerned, you owe them three years' worth of copy.' Then, her chin in her hands, 'So, you are dating?'

'No, Gemma.'

'Sorry, not convinced. A girl doesn't get that kind of glow without some serious attention from a man who lights up her soul.'

Max did not light up her soul. She wasn't that kind of fool. Every other part of her, maybe…

'I've been taking vitamins,' she said.

'What kind? I want some.' Then, 'Really not dating?'

'You mean the institution where a man asks a woman out, takes her out to a concert or for a meal or whatever he believes is the fastest way between her sheets?'

Gemma nodded expectantly.

'No. I'm not doing that.'

It was true.

Dating was part of the getting-to-know-you ritual in which a couple circled around each other, tested each other against their own lives to see if they were a fit. Or, failing that, whether the sexual attraction was powerful enough to counteract common sense…at least for the time being.

With Max it wasn't like that.

They didn't have to play that game. They'd known each other all their lives. Why waste time sitting opposite one another in a fancy restaurant where the whole world could see them making small talk and leap to its own conclusions, when they could be sharing supper in bed? Why waste time providing gossip for the tabloid diary writers?

Besides, the secrecy added a certain piquancy, an extra level of excitement to their affair.

'You're smiling again,' Gemma said.

'I can't think why when I'm still waiting for those drawings.'

'They haven't arrived yet.' Then, turning her head as someone came into the outer office, 'Correction, the boss has brought them himself.'

'Max?'

Louise saw the exact moment when Gemma realised the truth. Not that she said anything. She didn't have to. She looked at Max standing in the doorway, holding not just the large envelope containing drawings of the Qu'Arim restaurant, but a spray of dusky pink roses, glanced back at Louise and then pointedly removed herself from the office, closing the door behind her.

'Were all the couriers busy?' Louise asked as he dropped the roses on her desk.

'The message I'm delivering is far too personal to entrust with a spotty youth on a motorcycle.'

His hands braced on the arms of her chair, he bent to kiss her, taking his time about it.

The thrill, the tiny shock of delight, was still as new, as startling as the first kiss they'd shared. It made her feel like a giddy eighteen-year-old. And as old and knowing as time.

He pulled back an inch. 'Besides, I'm on my way to talk to the accountants.'

'And you decided to take the long way round?'

He grinned, propped himself on the desk. 'Not because I need the exercise.'

'Oh, please, I'm not complaining,' she said, laughing. 'But I fear that we've just been rumbled.'

'Rumbled?' He glanced at the closed door. 'Gemma?'

'I think the flowers might have been the give-away.'

'A gift from a grateful employer.' Then, 'What, Oliver Nash never sent you flowers?' he asked, glancing at the vast arrangement that had been delivered to the office, a personal thank-you for the HOTfood launch.

'He sends Flowers,' she said, emphasising the capital F with a broad gesture that suggested vast quantities of hothouse blooms. 'And they are delivered by messenger. He doesn't drop by with a bunch of roses from the flower seller on the corner.'

'His mistake.' He grinned, looked at the roses. 'Although I didn't set out with flowers in mind, I have to admit. It was just when I saw these they reminded me of you.'

'You needed reminding?'

She picked them up, ruffled the velvety petals beneath her fingers and then, aware that he was waiting for her to ask in what way exactly they had reminded him of her she looked up, inviting him to elaborate.

'Reminded me specifically of the moment when you dropped your dress at your feet. They're exactly the colour of the incredibly small amount of underwear you were wearing, wanton hussy that you are—'

'Sh!' she said, her face turning the same colour as the roses.

'A wanton hussy who blushes like a schoolgirl.'

'I don't!'

He didn't argue, just reached out, hand closed, and rubbed her hot cheek with the back of his fingers.

'Is it such a big deal, Lou? Gemma knowing? People saw us dining with Patsy and Derek last week.'

'No one we knew.'

'Maybe not. But the *maître d'* recognised me and when one Valentine eats in a restaurant that's not his own, it's gossip. When two of us do it, it's news. You're not exactly low profile, Lou, and Patsy didn't opt for discretion in her choice of restaurants. She wanted to show you off.'

Louise groaned. 'I know. Half the staff at that place are probably Diary stringers for the redtops, but I couldn't bear to disappoint her when she was so excited.'

'No, of course you couldn't.'

'From now on we'll have to be more discreet.'

'Will we?'

'Please, Max,' she said, imploring him to understand.

'You have a problem being seen out with me?' He

shook his head. He was still smiling, but not right up to his eyes. 'And I thought the reason we stayed in was because you couldn't get enough of my body.'

'Well,' she said, desperate to tease him back to a smile, 'there's an upside to everything,'

'But?'

'But nothing. I don't care about other people, Max, only Dad. He's just getting over his heart attack…'

'And you think if he knew that I was sleeping with his little princess the shock would kill him?'

'I'm not… I'm not prepared to take the risk, are you?' she said, flaring up briefly at his lack of sympathy. Then, silently begging him to understand. This affair was too hot to sustain itself for long; it would burn itself out in its own heat soon enough… 'You know how he feels about your father.'

'Bitter. Chip on his shoulder a mile high.' Max was not with her on this one. 'But I'm not my father. Besides, don't you think he should have got over that at his age?'

'Try to understand, Max. Your father was the son of an adored second wife while my father saw his own mother abandoned, without support, dying of pneumonia.'

'The country was at war, Louise. Life was hard for everyone.' Then, 'It's not just that, though, is it?'

She shook her head. 'No. Your father had everything. Not just two loving parents, but looks, charisma, women falling at his feet.'

'Children of his own?'

'Sons,' she said, the word like a knife to her heart. But even as she said the word she finally understood why her father had wanted to keep the fact that she was adopted a secret. No, not so much a secret as sweeping it under the carpet. Pretending it wasn't so. Because even in this, most basic of human functions, he'd been eclipsed by his younger, more glamorous half brother…

He'd never been able to forgive his father for being there for Robert. Caring more about Robert. Never able to forgive Robert for having everything.

Was she falling into the same mistake? Unable to forgive, to move on?

He didn't deserve that from her.

'He's finally caught up in the son stakes,' Max reminded her.

She shook her head.

'But even in that he was deprived, don't you see? He didn't know they existed until last year. He blamed William Valentine for that, too.'

He shrugged. 'To be honest I have more sympathy with your mother. Have you been to see her recently?'

She shook her head.

'She needs you, Lou. No matter how much you enjoy Patsy's company, Ivy's your mother too.'

'You think she'd understand…this? Us? Approve?'

'Like Patsy, you mean?'

Maybe that was why she'd enjoyed the evening with Patsy so much. She hadn't judged them. They hadn't had to hide their feelings from her.

'As my mother, Max. As John Valentine's wife.'

'The reason Patsy isn't bothered, Lou, is because she hasn't been involved. There's no history.'

'That's not true!'

'For Ivy, you're her whole life. Talk to her, Louise.'

'Not about us,' she said, not wanting to go there. Determined to keep him with her on this one thing. 'This isn't…'

'Isn't what?'

She shook her head. 'Serious,' she said, opting for the easy answer.

'Not serious?' There was a momentary pause. 'Are you telling me that you're just playing with me? That all you want is my body?'

'Absolutely,' she said, grabbing at this chance to turn it into a joke.

'Is that right?' He let the past go and, with an imperceptible contraction of the lines fanning out from the corners of his eyes, began a slow, seductive smile that made her forget all about her mother, her father, instead jolting her into one-hundred-per-cent awareness of him. 'Are you sure it isn't because being with me makes you feel just the tiniest bit…wicked?'

'Only "the tiniest bit"?' she managed, through a throat apparently stuffed with cobwebs. 'I was hoping for much better than that.'

His answer was to open his hand, cup her head, lean forward and kiss her, long and deep, his tongue a silky invader that ransacked her mouth, turning her limbs to water.

'Better?' he asked, when he'd done and she lay back, limp in her chair.

'Much better,' she said, smiling like an idiot in a way that would have confirmed all Gemma's darkest suspicions.

Blissfully better.

Her plan had been to gorge on a glut of Max Valentine so that she would lose her appetite for his kisses, his love, but the truth was that they were addictive; the more she had, the more she wanted.

With him she held nothing back. There was no reserve. He turned her on like a searchlight.

'So,' she said, her voice pure vamp, 'do you want to make out on my desk?'

He kissed her once more, but briefly, before straightening. 'While I'd love to stay and play, sweetheart, I've got an appointment that won't keep,' he said, backing towards the door, grinning. 'But hold that thought until our evening meeting. I'll see you on my desk at six-thirty…'

'You're walking out on me?' Okay, so she hadn't

actually meant it. Well, probably hadn't meant it. But no way was she letting him get away with that…

'It isn't easy,' he assured her, but he kept on walking.

She let him reach the door before she said, 'So you don't want to check that the underwear really does match the roses, then?'

He lost the grin. 'You're wearing it?'

'There's only one way to find out.'

When he'd gone, Gemma appeared in the doorway. 'Max was in a hurry.'

'He was late for an appointment with the accountant.'

Believing her had been his first mistake; coming back to check for himself had been his second.

Two out of three wasn't bad.

She'd felt the need to test her power, make it as hard as humanly possible for him to leave, but he'd eventually managed to tear himself away. Late, it was true, but still not here. Not that she should be surprised. Max had always taken his responsibilities seriously. Put Bella Lucia before anything—anyone—else. It was, now she understood him a little better, easier to see why.

'So?' Gemma picked up the roses. 'Do these go in water or the bin?' She sniffed them, pulled a face. 'They've got no scent,' she said, as if that settled it.

'Max didn't buy them for the scent.' And her

smile returned as she remembered exactly why he'd bought them. For the moment he was finding more than enough time for pleasure. 'Put them in water, Gem. I'll have them on my desk.'

Next time he called in, he'd see them there and he'd remember, too.

She caught herself. Next time? She shook her head as if to clear it. Enjoy the moment, she reminded herself. Enjoy each time he broke stride, found precious time to be with her.

Then she smiled. She might not have been able to do more than delay him but she'd done a very satisfactory job of distracting him. The image she'd planted in his head, her scent, the taste of her, would be with him all the time he was with the accountant, discussing the costs for fitting out and launching Bella Lucia in Meridia.

When Gemma returned with the vase, she lingered, fussing with the flowers until Louise put down her pen, sat back and said, 'Okay. You've obviously got something on your mind. Out with it.'

'It's nothing.' Then, finally, she looked at her. 'Just… You will be careful, Lou?'

'Careful? Is this where I get the "safe sex" lecture?'

'Well, if you think you need a refresher course, but to be honest I was more concerned about your heart. Max Valentine is not exactly Mr Commitment, is he?'

'That's not fair!' Louise responded without thinking. Defending him. Who, in all his life, had ever been one hundred per cent committed to him? Put him first?

Then, as Gemma's eyebrows hit the ceiling and she realised that she'd overdone it, she tried to limit the damage.

'I'm not looking for commitment,' she said. And it was true, she wasn't. Hadn't been… 'This thing between Max and me…'

How to explain it to Gemma? Impossible when she wasn't entirely sure what it was herself. It had all seemed so simple…

'This "thing"?' Gemma prompted, making quote marks that suggested scepticism, if not downright sarcasm.

No, it *was* simple.

'It's not serious. Really,' she stressed when her PA, who knew her far too well to be easily fooled, did not look convinced. 'It's just unfinished business, that's all. Something that's been simmering away since we were adolescents. It should have happened a long time ago. Would have if we'd known the truth, that I was adopted. That there was no impediment to a relationship.'

'So all that snapping and snarling at one another was no more than repressed lust and now, what, you're just getting it—getting him—out of your system?'

'You see? Easy,' she said, with more conviction than she actually felt. It had been so heart-stoppingly special to look up, see him there. 'It's no more than a bit of fun,' she insisted.

Gemma was looking at her a little oddly and even as she said the words she knew, deep down, that it had gone way beyond that.

But it was a temporary madness. It had to be. She'd given herself until the fourteenth. On that day all debts would be paid and by then Max Valentine would be out of her system, as Gemma had so neatly put it.

'So why be coy?' her PA persisted. 'It's not as if either of you are involved with anyone else. Max is apparently wedded to his job and it's been nearly three years since you split up with—'

Louise stopped her with an impatient gesture. She didn't want to think about James, let alone talk about him.

'Dad's had enough shocks lately, don't you think? You know the history.'

She'd spilled it all to Gemma, needing someone completely neutral to talk to after her father had blurted out that she was adopted. It was Gemma who'd held the tissues, poured the brandy, found out how to trace her real mother.

'I can see that your dad wouldn't be exactly thrilled by the idea of you and Max as an item,' Gemma admitted, 'but neither of you are kids…'

'No. We're not. I told you, it's no more than a…' Louise made a vague gesture, unable to say the words again.

'A bit of fun,' Gemma said, obligingly filling in the blanks for her.

'So,' she said. 'You must see why we're not broadcasting it.'

'And Max feels that way too?'

Her PA was nothing if not persistent. 'You were the one who pointed out his commitment problem.'

'So I did.' Then, brightly, 'And actually I do understand, boss. If I was having "a bit of fun" with a man who put an urgent appointment with his accountant ahead of some hot lunchtime sex, I wouldn't want anyone to know, either.'

'Gemma!'

'No, honestly, your secret is safe with me,' she said, grinning wickedly, 'although next time you might try—'

'Enough!'

'Only trying to help,' she said, turning to go. Then, turning back, 'Just do yourself a favour, Lou, and remember that while Max Valentine is undoubtedly having fun—' She held up her hands '—okay, okay, you're *both* having fun,' she went on quickly before Louise could interrupt. 'But when it's all over, when he's got you out of *his* system, he'll be able to walk away without a backward glance.'

Once she would have believed that, before he'd opened up to her about his mother, his childhood. Not just that painfully cryptic moment on the plane but in the quiet moments of intimacy he'd somehow been able to respond to her queries about how things had gone with a frankness that had shown her a new side of his character. She knew that the charming, untouchable, totally in control Max Valentine had a vulnerability that she suspected no one else had ever seen.

But she was vulnerable, too, hiding inside her own shell, and with an archness she was far from feeling she said, 'Are you suggesting that I won't?'

'All I'm saying, Louise, is that it's taken you three years to get over James Cadogan. I very much doubt that you're a woman who can do detached "fun".'

'Gem—'

'It's okay, lecture over,' Gemma said, backing off. 'I'm going to get a sandwich. Can I bring anything for you?'

'Please,' she said, relieved to be moving into safer territory. 'Salmon,' she said. 'And a blueberry yoghurt.'

'Anything else?'

A chance to do things again, perhaps. Max had been casual enough about her need for secrecy, but he didn't like it. It wasn't as if they were doing anything wrong, anything they need be ashamed of.

They were together and, no matter how temporary their affair was intended to be, in some deep, hidden recess of her soul, she knew she wanted the world to know, to see what they had.

'Lou?'

She shook her head. 'Nothing.' Nothing anyone could give her.

'I've got confirmation of an article in a heavyweight international financial journal today, Max. The package I put together of the Qu'Arim restaurant sold it to them.'

'Mmm?'

He was engrossed in a booking list and only gave Louise half his attention.

She reached over and removed the sheet of paper he was working on and when he looked up, she kissed him. Only when he was kissing her back did she pull away. 'It's half past six, Max. My time.'

He leaned back, squeezed the space between his eyes. Smiled at her. 'You look good enough to eat.'

'That is not out of the question. First, business.'

'A financial journal?' he said, just to demonstrate that he'd been listening. 'Why would they be interested in us?'

'The first new Bella Lucia in twenty-five years may only be of passing interest to the kind of people who make their global deals over lunch at the

Mayfair restaurant,' she began. 'Something to note for the next time they're in Qu'Arim—'

'Only of passing interest?'

Question the interest quotient of his precious restaurants and suddenly she had his attention.

'So what's the big deal?' he asked.

'The big deal is not a single restaurant, but that it's the first in a new era of expansion. This magazine is read by people who know us, trust us, show it by coming here to make their deals in the discreet atmosphere of the Mayfair restaurant. They can smooth our path overseas, Max. They'll come to us with partnership proposals, finance.' Then, when he didn't immediately congratulate her for being brilliant, 'Tell me if you think I'm stepping on your toes again, Max.' Then, more concerned at how tired he looked than that he wasn't interested in what she had to say, 'If you're really too busy to spare me half an hour this evening?'

'No, no...' He dragged his fingers through hair that already bore the evidence of previous abuse. 'Really. Tell me about it.'

'I'll make an appointment for you to meet with their features writer,' she continued. 'In the meantime they want pictures, not just of you but of Dad and your father, too. I've organised that for tomorrow. Here. The Mayfair restaurant will be familiar—'

'For goodness sake, Lou, we've only just managed to shoehorn the pair of them out to pasture. Give them an inch—'

'Relax. You'll be front and centre, but the features writer will want some background on William Valentine, personal memories. How he built his empire from scratch after the war, when there was still rationing.' She smiled. 'They like men who can overcome apparently insurmountable obstacles to make things happen. And three generations of Valentines make us look solid.'

'We are solid.'

'I know, but trust me on this, Max. It'll look good.'

'Yes, of course it will. Sorry.' Then, 'You've spoken to your father?'

'No, I was busy. Gemma organised it all.'

'Lou…' He got up, put his arms around her, pulled her close. 'You can't go on punishing them like this. They love you.'

'They lied to me.'

'They were afraid.'

'They were?' She pulled back. Looked up at him. 'Why?'

'They were afraid that you wouldn't love them as much if they weren't your own parents.'

'But that's…' She was going to say that it was ridiculous. But he'd had stepmothers who'd had children of their own. For whom he was just a tiresome add-on. How had that felt? 'You're right,' she said. 'I just need a little more time.'

'Don't leave it too long.' Then, gesturing at the paperwork on his desk, taking the crumpled paper from her own hand, 'Let me get this straight and we'll go and have a drink.' He pulled a face as he returned to his chair. 'I'll need a drink.'

'What are you doing?' she asked, looking over his shoulder and felt a sharp chill. 'Oh, you're working on Valentine's Day.'

Huge tips from goofily happy men and a fabulous party afterwards to celebrate the anniversary of the opening of the Chelsea restaurant on Valentine's Day in nineteen forty-six. It was a magic occasion. And this year was their diamond jubilee, so they were pulling out all the stops.

'It's next week,' he said, looking up at her as if he wanted to say something. Thinking better of it.

He didn't have to say it. They both knew that the fourteenth was her own self-imposed deadline.

'How are we doing?' she asked.

'Booked to the rafters. All that stuff about us in last week's *City Lights* seems to have made everyone crazy to celebrate with us.'

'It's word association, Max.' He looked up. 'The juxtaposition of diamonds and Valentine's Day. It was an easy sell.' Then, 'Maybe you should insist that all the men are going to be packing the real thing before we accept their bookings.' Max frowned. 'We don't want any of our female diners to go home disappointed.'

'You're talking about engagement rings?'

'Well, obviously.'

'Wouldn't that rather spoil the surprise?'

'If an unmarried woman gets taken out to dinner at Bella Lucia on Valentine's Day, the only surprise will be if there isn't a ring hidden in the dessert. What could be described as a dumb-male, tears-before-bedtime scenario.'

He laughed. 'Right.' Then, sitting back, easing his neck. 'Would you believe that I've never had a Valentine's Day date?'

'No.'

'It's true. There's never been a Valentine's Day when I haven't had to work. From the day I turned eighteen and was old enough to serve a drink, it was the one night I had to turn up and pitch in.'

'Well, that's one way of avoiding matrimony,' she agreed, dropping a kiss on his forehead. 'You're clearly too busy to talk marketing and PR tonight. Let's give it a miss.'

'No…' He reached out, caught her hand. 'You could stay and help. It is all your fault that we're overwhelmed.'

'Thanks, but I'll pass on that one.'

'You could just stay and let me look at you.'

'Tempting, but once you get drawn into the nitty-gritty of how much chocolate, how much champagne you're going to need, you'll forget I'm here.'

For a moment she thought he might protest. Thought he might abandon planning the biggest night of their year and take her for that drink he'd offered. Instead he dragged his fingers through his hair, and, his attention already back on the complex planning required to ensure that everything ran smoothly, he said, 'You're right. I'll see you later.'

No. She should say no. Begin to ease away now while she still could...

'If I'm asleep...' she said, putting a spare set of keys on his desk and instead of taking a step back, keeping their relationship at a level where just sleeping together was enough, she said, 'Don't wake me.'

Max picked up the keys, watched her gather her things, smile back at him as she headed for the door, hating to see her go. She brightened his day, had changed his life in ways he couldn't begin to understand. It gave him a new kind of strength, and yet it frightened the life out of him, too. He'd surrendered something to her, lost the one thing that had kept him together even during the blackest times. Control.

'Louise...' She paused, turned back. 'About the Valentine's party...'

He'd been doing his best not to think about the huge party the family threw each year, after the restaurants closed—a celebration, a thank-you to all the staff. All day, as he'd been working on the plans for that evening, he'd remembered their deal, that she planned to draw a line under her involvement on that day…

'What about it?' she asked.

'You will be there?'

She hesitated. He almost thought her shoulders sagged a little. Then she nodded.

'Sure, Max,' she said. 'I might even dance with you.'

'Uncle Robert!' Louise dropped her briefcase on Max's desk, kissed his father, bestowed the kind of brief, distant smile on Max that she'd always used around her family. His eyebrows rose a touch, he held her gaze for a moment longer than felt right, but then just nodded. Let it be. And that felt wrong, too. This was all wrong. She should go to him, kiss him…

'How's Aunt Bev?' she asked, turning to Max's father.

'Good. She sends her love,' he said. 'Your father isn't with you?'

'He's making his own way here.' She glanced at her watch. 'The photographer isn't due for another fifteen minutes…' She turned as the door opened behind her

Her father had lost weight since his heart attack. Had been taking exercise, watching his diet. He looked fitter than he had done in a long time, she thought.

Fitter and angrier.

He was carrying a folded newspaper and, ignoring her, he walked up to Max and slapped it against his chest.

'Do you want to tell me what's going on?'

'John…'

John Valentine silenced his brother with a look. 'He's a man. Let him speak for himself. Well?' he demanded.

Max had caught the paper before it fell and, without answering, looked at it. Said one brief word.

'"Kissing Cousins?"' John Valentine demanded as Max offered the paper to Louise so that she could see for herself.

It was just a single paragraph in the diary column of the *London Courier*.

Headed, Kissing Cousins? it said:

We are delighted to learn that our favourite PR consultant, Louise Valentine, is back in the family fold. Relations have been somewhat strained, apparently, since the disclosure that Louise was adopted. All is now peace and harmony, however, and she's putting her talents to good use, working with her cousin Max Valentine to promote the family's exclusive Bella Lucia restaurants.

Louise, who was once a regular girl-about-town and closely linked with the Hon James Cadogan—soon to be married to former model Charlotte Berkeley—has, in recent years, devoted all her energies to building her own business. Max, rarely without a beauty on his arm and frequently seen playing in the Sultan of Qu'Arim's polo team, has also dropped out of the social scene to concentrate on ambitious expansion plans overseas.

The couple, who were recently spotted dining together with Louise's birth mother, the lively Patsy Simpson Harcourt and her new husband, are said to be inseparable, although they're keeping their romance low-key at the moment. We wish them both well.

'Said?' she demanded. 'Who said? No one…'

Louise barely stopped herself from letting slip her own version of Max's expletive, but it was too late. She'd already confirmed her father's worst fears.

'Well, I don't have to ask if it's true. I've only got to look at you.'

'Daddy…' The childish word slipped out, maybe

because that was exactly how she felt. Like a child who'd disappointed her father.

'I'm not blaming you, Louise.'

Blaming her!

'I realise you've been knocked for six by everything that's happened and he's clearly taken advantage of you when you're in a vulnerable—'

'Would someone mind telling me what the hell is going on?' Robert demanded.

Louise handed the paper to her uncle without a word, but he didn't get a chance to read for himself before his brother rounded on him.

'What's going on?' John demanded. He took a step closer. 'What's going on? You have to ask? He's your son,' he said, pointing at Max, 'and the apple doesn't fall very far from the tree. Ask him what's going on!'

'Dad! Please.' Louise reached for her father's arm, concerned for him. 'Did you travel into town on your own?'

'Of course I travelled on my own. I've been commuting between Richmond and Mayfair all my working life. I don't need a minder to hold my hand.'

'You haven't been well. Maybe I should call Mum…'

But before she could reach her cell phone, he took the hand she'd laid on his arm and tucked it firmly against him, pulling her close, as if to protect her.

'Like father, like son,' he said, still looking at his brother. 'Max will play with Louise's feelings, destroy her. William Valentine all over again. You're just like your father, Robert—'

'William Valentine was your father, too.'

'Just like your father,' John Valentine repeated. 'And your son is just like you. You can't be trusted around a decent woman, any of you.'

'Well, I don't know about that,' Robert drawled. 'I'll admit to having had more than my fair share of wives, but I'm not a hypocrite. At least I married the mothers of my children, all of them, and while I may not have been the best father in the world, I never lied to them. They knew who their parents were.'

John released Louise and lunged at his brother, grabbing him by the lapels of his jacket, holding him as if he wanted to shake him.

'Dad!'

Max and Louise said the word in unison. Neither of them took the slightest notice, but as Louise leapt in to separate them Max caught her, held her back.

'Leave them,' he said as she tried to shake him off. 'It's time they settled it.'

'Well, what are you waiting for, big brother?' Robert sneered, provocatively, before she could answer. 'Go on, hit me. Heaven alone knows you've wanted to do it for long enough. Why don't you relax that stiff upper lip for once in your life and take a swing at me?'

CHAPTER NINE

FOR a moment nothing happened. Then, as his brother shuddered, eased the vice-like grip on his jacket, Robert said, 'Let it go, John. Let it go.'

'How can I? Our father stole my sons from me! Bought off their mother, kept me in ignorance to save a scandal.'

'He acted from the best of motives. You'd just married Ivy. He was so proud...' Robert shook his head. 'He was always so proud of you. You were the good son, the one who made a good marriage, brought honour to his house with your rich, well-connected bride—'

'I married for love.'

'The rest was just a bonus?'

For a moment Louise thought her father would take up his brother's invitation and hit him.

'No!' she cried.

For a moment John seemed beyond hearing, but then he almost visibly pulled himself together and taking a step back from the brink, released his grip on his brother's jacket. 'Ivy…' His face softened. 'In my marriage, I've been the most fortunate of men.'

'Ivy has been the most fortunate of women, John.' For a moment Robert's devil-may-care features were haunted by something very like regret, then, brushing it aside, he said, 'Dad didn't want anything to spoil that for you. Your boys never went without. He didn't abandon them, the way he abandoned you.'

'But I did,' John replied. 'I did…'

As Louise let out a small sound that echoed her father's anguish Max drew her close and she didn't hesitate as she turned her face into his shoulder, knowing that his only concern was for her.

'I didn't know…' her father said.

'Blame their mother for that if you must blame someone,' Robert told him, unmoved. 'She didn't want you in her life. Made the decision not to tell you about the twins. Face it, John, if her singing career hadn't flopped, if she hadn't decided that marriage to you was the soft option, no one would ever have known about your boys.'

'She was in trouble. She had a right to my help. He should have told me, Robert. He got it wrong,' John said, finally letting go. 'But then he didn't ever really know me. He didn't want to. You were his joy. The one with a true flair for the business he loved, while I was just a glorified accountant. The truth is, I made him feel guilty.'

Robert didn't dispute it and Louise saw her father's shoulders sag a little. Felt an ache for the boy he'd been, the man he'd become. Family, but always just a little bit on the outside. Like Max, she thought. And like Max, needing to be in control of everything, refusing to allow anything to deflect them, disturb the even tenor of their lives. And it was Max, regarding his father, his uncle, with something like despair, whom she turned to, reached out to.

'And because he didn't learn from his own mistakes,' she heard her father say, 'I've been put through the same wringer.'

'I'm not excusing him—'

John and Robert Valentine, still fighting a sixty-year-old battle, did not even notice them as Max took her hand, held it, drew her closer, put his arm around her.

'No?' John glared at him. 'It sounds very much like it.'

'Well, maybe. You're right about a lot of things. He was uncomfortable with you and I can understand why you resented me. But what happened in the past, to you, to your mother, was not my fault.'

'You had it so easy. You were so spoiled…'

'Maybe that's why I'm not the man you are, John.'

John didn't appear to hear him. 'My mother

suffered so much. I sat and watched her die and I couldn't do anything.'

'It was a terrible thing for a boy to go through.'

For a moment Louise thought Robert was going to put his arm around his brother in a gesture of comfort.

'Yes…' she whispered, urging him to do it, for the two men to forgive each other so that they could move on. In response, Max pulled her a little closer.

Forgiveness.

John and Robert weren't the only ones who needed to find that in their hearts. As she felt all the hurt, that terrible sense of betrayal fell away from her. Her father loved her. Why else would he be angry with Max? Nothing else mattered… She had to tell him that so that they could all move on.

Robert clearly thought better of such an unrestrained gesture, but put his hand on his brother's shoulder. 'A terrible thing,' he repeated. 'But it wasn't anyone's fault that your mother died, John. Everyone was short of food. There was no penicillin. Even if he'd been there, instead of away fighting, Dad couldn't have done anything to save her. You must know that.'

'He shouldn't have stopped loving her.' Her father looked desperate.

'People can't help their feelings, John.' And he looked across at Max, as if he, too, was asking for something, some understanding.

'She was his wife!' He shook off his brother's hand. 'What would you know about fidelity?' And he took a step back, turned to her. 'Don't you see, Louise?' he said, pointing at Max. 'It's what Valentine men do. William, Robert with an endless succession of wives, Max with his string of girlfriends.' Then, letting his hand fall, 'And me, too.' The fire went out of him. 'Robert's right. I'm no different.'

'No, Dad...' she said, hating to see him in so much pain. To see him blaming himself. If she'd been there, hadn't been so wrapped up in her own hurt...

He brushed her protest aside. 'I had an affair, moved on and never looked back, never gave the girl another thought in forty years. Had twin boys who never knew their father...'

'It wasn't like that. You didn't know—'

'I should have known. It's something in us, Louise. The Valentine gene. Max has got his arm around you now, but it won't last. He'll stop loving you. He might not mean to hurt you, but he won't be able to help himself.'

'No!'

No more secrets. No more lies. Especially not to herself. She didn't know what the future held for Max and her; all she knew was that hidden away their relationship didn't stand a chance. 'You're better than that.' Then, in a gesture that no one could mistake, she took Max's hand in hers and, standing at his side, said, 'You're better than that, Daddy. And so is Max. Tell him, Uncle Robert. Tell him!'

'Louise is right, John. He's not like me,' Robert said. 'Max, Jack, the girls, I don't know how it happened when I was such a screw-up as a father, but they've all turned out better than me.'

But John couldn't let it go.

'No...' He shook his head as if to deny what was before him. 'I've seen you hurting, Lou. When you and James split up I thought my heart would break, too. I know you've never got over it.'

'No, it wasn't—'

'You're my little girl and your pain is my pain.' A sigh escaped him. 'I've loved you since the moment we brought you home, loved you more than any words can say, but I should have tried, should have told you. Daniel and Dominic are special, very special to me, but you are my most precious daughter. No blood tie could be stronger.' He reached out, covered her hand, the one holding onto Max, with his own. 'No one could ever replace you.'

'I know, Dad.' She looked at Max, smiled at him. He knew the pain of family breakdown, but he understood the true value of family, too. She'd have lost that but for him. In every way that mattered, John Valentine was her father.

She kissed Max, just to show him that nothing, no one, could keep them apart, and then she stepped forward, put her arms around her father, gave him the hug she should have found it in her heart to give him months ago, when he'd been hurting, when he'd needed her most. 'You don't have to tell me,' she said, her eyes full of tears. 'I understand.'

She'd been so afraid that Max was trying to drag her back, keep her from her new family, but she'd been wrong. She'd thought he'd been trying to control her when all he'd wanted was to show her that she didn't have to choose, that she could have both; made certain that she didn't throw away the family, the life, she had. One could, it seemed, never have too much family as far as Max was concerned.

'I may have forgotten for a little while,' she said, 'but I've always known. I'm sorry I haven't been a better daughter. So sorry…'

'No, no. Hush… It's all right. I understood. Just, tell your mother…' He looked at her. 'We both need to tell your mother how much we love her. This has been so hard on her.'

As he said the word—love—she couldn't stop herself from looking at Max and she knew that she'd been fooling herself. There was no way she was ever going to get Max Valentine out of her system. He wasn't just 'unfinished business'. He was part of her. Without him she could never be whole.

It wasn't some *coup de foudre*, a blinding realisation that she was in love with him, but rather an acknowledgement of the fact that she'd been in love with him all her life and, although the words were for her father, she looked at Max as she said, 'Promise me that you won't blame Max for what has happened between us. He didn't take advantage of me. I was the one who wanted this,' she said. 'Wanted him. I always did. Even before I understood the feelings.' She was laying her heart bare to him. Trusting him. 'It may not last. There are no guarantees, but at last we're able to know one another in ways that we once thought impossible. That's more than I ever hoped for.'

'Impossible?' As her father realised what she was saying, he groaned. 'Because you believed you were blood relations?' He shook his head. 'Then that's my fault, too…'

'Don't! The past is gone. Now, today, is all that matters. Tomorrow, next week, who knows? Only that the future is ours and, whether we make or break it, it's our joint responsibility. It takes two to build a partnership.'

'But only one to break it.' For a moment her father continued to glare at Max. Then, with the slightest shrug, he said, 'Heaven help you if you do anything to hurt her.'

'No one can say what the future will bring, Uncle

John, but maybe you should trust Louise to make her own decisions. Believe me, she's more than capable of taking care of herself. I've just had a grandstand demonstration of where she learned that fly-off-the-handle temper.'

Robert Valentine laughed. 'He's got you there, John.'

'I haven't got a quick temper,' Louise declared, roundly, then, recalling her father's recent heart scare, she said, 'Dad! Are you okay?'

'Okay? Of course I'm okay. Why shouldn't I be…?' And then he too recalled that he was supposed to be taking it easy, not getting excited, and clapped his heart to his chest. 'It's okay,' he said, grinning as he saw their concerned faces. 'It's still beating.' Then, 'But, um, better not tell your mother about that little outburst, eh? She'll only make a fuss.'

Louise flung her arms around her father's neck. 'Idiot,' she murmured in his ear. 'I do love you.'

He hugged her back, said, 'Then do something for me.'

Give up Max? Please, no, don't ask that. Not now…

'I know how much I've hurt you, Louise. I'm only just beginning to see how much my foolish pride, my need for secrecy, has cost you, but I'm to blame, not your mother. Stop punishing her. Live the day God has given you.' Then, standing back to look at her, 'If this last few months have taught me anything, it's that.'

'I'm learning,' she said, glancing at Max. Mouthed a silent 'thank you' to him. He gave the slightest shake of the head, as if it was nothing to do with him, but she knew better.

The fact that they were here today was because he'd pursued her, refused to take no for an answer.

It was because of him that she was no longer alone and it was his hand she reached for as she said, 'I'll call Mum, talk to her, I promise. Today.'

Satisfied, and having given Max a look that told him in no uncertain terms that, whatever Louise had said, he'd be held responsible for any pain, John turned to his brother.

'How do you feel on that subject?'

Robert, who'd been brushing down his jacket, smoothing his rumpled lapels, looked up. 'What subject is that?'

'Living the day. Life being a one-time offer.'

'I wouldn't gamble on getting a second crack at it,' he agreed.

'Then I'd suggest it's time we stopped fighting past battles and made the most of what we have while we can enjoy it.'

Putting the word to the deed, he extended his hand, every inch the Englishman in the manner in which he formally declared an end to hostilities.

Robert, as much his father's son as John, took it, held it. Then, his Italian mother's genes rushing to the fore, he threw his arms around his brother and was still hugging him when the restaurant rang up to tell them that the photographer had arrived.

Max couldn't take his eyes off Louise as she talked to the photographer, made sure that she got exactly what she wanted. Totally professional. Once she turned and saw him watching her, flicked a strand of hair behind her ear, smiled right back.

It was the look of a supremely confident woman and as she turned to her father, settled his tie, laughed at something he said to her, he felt as if he'd lost her.

Not physically. She'd made her feelings public. But she'd stepped back inside the charmed circle, to a place where he couldn't follow.

After the photographer had gone and their respective parents put the word to the deed by staying to have lunch together, Louise and Max were left alone in the office.

'I ought to go,' she said.

She felt churned up, oddly vulnerable, her nerve endings exposed by so much raw emotion. It wasn't just John and Robert Valentine making their peace after so long, or even her own accord with her father; she now realised that while she'd laid her heart on the line, Max had said nothing. She needed to think about that. What it meant.

'I've got a pile of stuff waiting at the office and time is running out.'

'Nothing that won't keep for an hour.' Taking her hesitation for agreement, he said, 'We could both do with a little fresh air after this morning's melodrama. As the boss I'm taking an executive decision to go for a walk in the park.'

'You're not my boss, Max,' Louise said, matching his flippancy as she took her long scarlet coat from the stand. 'You're a charity case.'

'I think we need to talk about that,' he said, not rising to this provocation. 'The kiss covered until the fourteenth and you've done a great job. Now we have to discuss the future. What kind of retainer it's going to take to keep you as Bella Lucia's PR consultant.'

She glanced up at him as he took her coat, held it out for her. Nothing in his face gave her a clue whether that was all he wanted from her.

'I'm very expensive.'

'I'm sure, between us, we can hammer out some kind of financial package.'

'No discounts for family,' she said, her heart slipping into her boots as she let him ease her into her coat. 'The "kiss" deal was a one-time offer.' Like life, she thought, but when he didn't answer this echo of her father's words rang hollow in her ears.

'You should have brought some bread for the ducks,' she said as fifteen minutes later they skirted the lake in St James's Park. When, despite his apparent desire to talk, the silence had stretched to breaking-point.

'The greedy little beggars are too fat to fly as it is and, besides, I want your undivided attention.'

'We couldn't talk somewhere warm?' she asked.

'I want to ask you something. It's important. I don't want any ringing telephones, any distractions.'

She frowned. 'What? What is it?'

'I want to know what really happened between you and the Honourable James Cadogan.'

'James?' It was clear that Max had something on his mind, but that was the last thing she'd expected. 'He's ancient history,' she said, but uneasily.

'And yet the man's name crops up whenever you're mentioned. The *Courier* mentioned him today. And your father seemed to think I was catching you on the rebound, too. Taking advantage of your broken heart.'

'Oh, please.' If that was his problem, well, no problem… 'The *Courier* was simply rehashing the last piece of gossip they had on file, and as for Dad, well, reading it just reminded him what a failure as a daughter I am. Robert's daughter married a king, while I messed up my relationship with a simple 'honourable", a man who, I might add, my father thought would make the perfect son-in-law.'

'I don't think he was alone in that. I remember thinking at the time that if I heard his name connected to one more string of glowing adjectives I'd punch a hole in the wall.'

She managed a smile. 'I used to feel the same way when you were dating Sophie Blakiston. Whatever happened to her?'

'I didn't turn up once too often and she married an earl.'

'You don't learn, do you?'

'I didn't have much of an example in my old man.'

'No, it's not that. It isn't other women that tempt you away. You just love Bella Lucia more.'

'Now you're just trying to change the subject.'

Maybe, but he hadn't denied it.

'Of course I am,' she replied. 'No one likes to talk about their mistakes.'

'And what about James Cadogan? Was he a mistake?'

Louise, wanting him to let it go, said, 'Yes.' Then realising that this wasn't any better, 'No.' Then just shook her head.

'So why did you two break up?' Max persisted. 'Whatever happened then changed you. After Cadogan there's no one. It's like your personal life entered an ice age.'

'Stop trying to make it out to be such a big deal, Max. It came to a natural end. That's all.'

'No more than a light-hearted flirtation? That's odd, because, according to my mother, your mother was already drawing up the guest list for the wedding, choosing stationery for the invitations, talking designers for the dress—'

'Pure fantasy,' she said, but was unable to meet his steady gaze, couldn't bear the silence that told her plainer than words that Max was not convinced. She stopped, turned to face him. 'All right! It wasn't just fantasy. It was much more than that. Satisfied!'

He took her arm, continued walking. Waited.

'I was nearly thirty. Way past time for a girl to be married and producing babies, according to my mother, and, as she was quick to tell me, no one better was ever likely to come along. Not exactly the fairy tale, but no girl past the age of sixteen believes in those.'

Not if her Prince Charming of choice had a barbed-wire fence around him hung with warning notices saying 'do not touch'.

'So you were settling for the best you could get?'

'That's not fair to James. He *was* any girl's ideal husband. My mother was out of her mind with happiness; even my father approved.'

'The man must have been a saint,' he said, a touch acerbically. Then, 'Or was it because in the

fullness of time he'd have made Daddy's little girl
Lady Cadogan?'

'Now you're just being nasty. James was a
lovely man. Any father would have been delighted
with him as a son-in-law. Any woman would have
been lucky—'

'Methinks the lady doth protest too much.'

She shook her head, shivered.

An ice age…

Max stopped, removed the scarf he was wearing,
wrapped it around her neck, but didn't let go of the
ends, holding her within the circle of his arms and
instantly she felt warmer.

No ice there…

'So what went wrong?' he asked.

'Me,' she said. 'I told you.'

He frowned.

'What? You don't believe that? You don't
believe Little Miss Perfect capable of dumping
the best prospect for matrimonial bliss ever likely
to come her way?'

'You're mistaking me for someone else, Lou. I
never thought you were Little Miss Perfect.' His
eyes creased in one of those rare smiles that made
his eyes seem impossibly blue. A smile that assured
her he knew her far better than that. 'Daddy's Little
Princess is another matter.'

She laughed. He was the one person who'd

always been able to make her laugh. Before life, hormones, got in the way. How she'd missed that.

'Was I that bad?'

'Appalling,' he said, but with a smile. 'All frills, curls, and ponies. Once Jack and I lured you away on adventures, you weren't too bad. For a girl.'

'Thank you. I know you meant that as a compliment.'

'I knew you'd understand.' Then, releasing the scarf, he led the way to a bench that overlooked the lake and, with his arm around her waist, drew her close to keep her warm.

'So, Princess, tell me about Prince Charming.'

'I hoped you'd forgotten.'

'That bad?'

No more secrets…

'James did nothing wrong.' She sighed. 'He took all the flak from both families when it fell apart, but it was my fault, Max. All my fault.'

'Tell me,' he said.

She glanced at him. He raised his brows, an invitation to spill it all out. Get it off her chest.

'Trust me, Lou.'

'You won't sell my secrets to the *Courier* diary correspondent?' she said, in an attempt to make a joke of it.

'Trust me,' he repeated. No smile. No sexy little twitch of his eyebrows. He was in deadly earnest, now. Asking her to bare her soul to him. Expose her heart. Leave herself without anywhere to hide. *

To put her heart where her mouth had been half an hour earlier and demonstrate that she trusted him not to hurt her.

Maybe to prove that she wouldn't hurt him. That was an unexpected thought. She'd never seen Max as vulnerable in that way. His family had hurt him, but he'd never appeared deeply touched by any of his own romances…

No more secrets…

'It wasn't that I didn't try,' she said, looking across the lake, afraid to see the panic in his eyes as he realised what she was telling him. 'I wanted it to work. James really was perfect. Not just because there was a title in the offing, that the family owned half the county. He was really nice. Good. Kind. And he loved me.'

She turned to Max then, because she had to see his reaction. Had to know…

'We were going to announce our engagement on my birthday. Major party. Crates of champagne on order. My mother was ecstatic; my father was strutting around as if he owned the entire world.'

'So?'

'I tried, Max. I did all the right things, said all the right things and I thought it was going to work but in the end he said… James said…'

She felt trapped, laid bare in a way that simple nakedness could never expose her, but Max took her hand, held it, gave her his strength.

No more secrets, but it was so hard…

'He said that he loved me, wanted me to be his wife. He said he knew that I didn't feel those things as strongly as him, but that he'd accepted that. That he accepted that in a relationship there was always one person who loved more—'

'He must have had it bad,' he said, but not without sympathy.

'But not, apparently, fatally. He said that he could accept all that, but he was beginning to suspect that there was someone else.'

He turned to her. 'He thought you were cheating on him?' he said, with a deadly calm.

'No! No. He said… He said that when he was holding me it felt as if I was looking over his shoulder, scanning the horizon, waiting for someone just out of sight to ride to my rescue. He wanted me to talk about it. Reassure him, I suppose.'

'But you couldn't?'

'No. He was wrong, Max.' She stared at their hands, locked together. 'He was wrong to accept less than my whole heart under any circumstances, but I was wrong, too. I should never have let it go so far. I hurt him and I deeply regret that. A partnership should be an equal passion, don't you think?'

'I would hope for that.'

'Would you accept less?' she asked.

'If there was no other choice, if only one person will do, then there must be the temptation to accept what's on offer, hope for more in time,' he said, frowning. 'But it's not a deal I could live with. Not the kind of foundation for the kind of marriage I'd consider. The kind that will last a lifetime.'

'That was the point. He didn't have to work at loving me while I …'

While she had been settling for second best.

When she realised that Max was waiting for her to finish the sentence, she shook her head. 'Whatever I was doing, he deserved better than I was giving him.'

'Tell me about the other man. The one out of sight.'

She looked away, but he caught her chin, forced her to face him. And she didn't have to say the words. He knew.

'That's why there's been no one else?' he persisted.

'What would have been the point?'

'What indeed?' He got up, pulled her to her feet, tucked her arm firmly beneath his and continued walking.

That was it? She'd just performed open heart

surgery on herself and he shrugged it off as nothing. She glanced at him. He wasn't looking at her, but straight ahead, and all she had was his chiselled profile against the cold blue of the sky.

'So, this affair we're having is your way of getting me out of your hair, is it?' he asked.

'That's a rather cold way of putting it.'

'But I'm right? I get you and your talent until the fourteenth. After that, you're going to move on?'

'That was the plan,' she admitted, miserably.

'And is it working?'

She lifted her shoulders in the smallest of shrugs. 'Not yet.'

'No. I had much the same outcome in mind, but the truth is there's nothing cold about what's between us, Louise. There never has been. It's always been fire, never ice. So the question we have to ask our selves, you and I, is where do we go from here?'

'I'm rather enjoying "here",' she said.

She wasn't so certain about Max.

'Isn't that the point? We aren't "here" any more are we? No more secret affair. Everyone knows about us now. That already takes us somewhere else.'

'It must have been Patsy, don't you think?' she said, unable to give him a direct answer. She didn't know where they were going. Only that he was right. With exposure, the mutual admission that they were both on an escape mission, came a change of direction.

One that she wanted.

Watching her father and uncle reach out for each other had shown her the futility, the waste of hiding one's feelings. If what she and Max had was to grow, it needed light, air…

'She must have been the one who spilled the beans to the *Courier*,' she prompted, a little desperately, when he didn't answer.

'I imagine so. She had us pegged from the minute she saw us together and she does have something of a runaway mouth.' Then, 'Are you angry with her?'

'Why would I be angry? We left your father and mine having lunch together, taking a trip down memory lane and laughing about it. That's something I thought I'd never see.' And she smiled, because that was wonderful. 'Without her, it might never have happened.' Then, 'Without you, Max.'

He looked at her. 'Me? What did I do?'

'You refused to let me go.'

He didn't come back with some major declaration, merely said, 'So, now we've been outed, I guess you're going to expect a little more by way of entertainment than supper in bed?'

On the point of saying that she couldn't think of any more entertaining way of spending her evenings with him, she thought better of it. It was time to move on, be open.

'Infinitely more,' she said. Then, 'Are you going to be free tomorrow evening?'

'What's happening?'

'Several things. I've got a late meeting so I'll have to forgo our six-thirty debriefing, but I do happen to have a couple of tickets for the Royal Opera House charity gala. A client sent them to me. I was going to give them away but maybe it's time to take our relationship on its first real public outing.' Then, when he didn't immediately respond, 'I'm asking you out on a date, Max. If you don't say yes within the next thirty seconds I might just die of embarrassment.'

'What time do you want me to pick you up?'

She'd expected more reaction. Didn't he realise just how big a deal this was for her? Was she being a complete fool? About to ask him, she decided she didn't want to know and let it go.

'I'll have to meet you at the theatre. No later than seven-fifteen,' she warned. 'It's a royal performance so we'll all have to be seated before the Queen arrives.'

'Seven-fifteen.' He nodded. 'So, what would you like to do this evening?'

'I'm going to see my mother, remember?' Weirdly she felt only relief. 'Want to come?' she teased.

'Scared what she'll say about us? Want some protection?' he replied, picking up the beat.

'No!' Then, 'Well, maybe, just a bit.'

'She'll be so glad to see you, Lou, she wouldn't care if you'd dyed your hair green. Give her my love.'

'I will. But more importantly,' she said, 'I'll give her mine.' She hailed a passing cab, then lifted herself up on her toes, kissed his cold cheek. 'I'll see you tomorrow. Seven-fifteen.'

Max watched her go, a mixture of feeling churning around inside him. He'd had to know what the deal was with James. If she was really bouncing back, using the undeniable sexual charge between them, using him to wipe the other man from her mind.

Now he knew the truth. And it terrified the life out of him.

The world seemed like a freshly minted place and the evening positively sparkled as Louise stepped out of the taxi outside the theatre. She had spent the previous evening with her parents, talking about her adoption, about how putting off telling her the truth had gradually, without anyone actually making a decision, become a permanent situation. Because it hadn't seemed to matter. She was their daughter. Why complicate things?

It had seemed that simple.

But now together, they had faced up to the mistakes of the past and, as a family, were looking forward to a brighter happier future, she thought, smiling as she paid her fare, looked around, certain that Max would be there waiting for her. Or maybe he was already inside, a drink waiting…

Or then again, maybe not, she thought, after she'd fought her way through the crush to the bar and realised he wasn't there.

She glanced at her watch. It was okay. He had another five minutes. She bought a programme, glanced through it, conscious of being alone in a crowd in which everyone else had someone to talk to.

An announcement asked people to take their seats.

She went back outside. Took out her cellphone, checked for messages. Nothing.

She could ring him, but, actually, what was the point?

On the stroke of half past, she dropped the programme in the nearest litter bin and hailed a taxi.

Gemma put her head around the door. 'Have you got your mobile turned off, Lou? Max says he's been trying to get you since last night.'

'That can't be right. Max apparently doesn't know my mobile number.'

'Louise…'

'I'll say one thing for you, Max, you're consistent,' she said, not looking up from her desk. She heard the office door close as Gemma left them in private. 'And I'm dumb. You've been standing me up since I was sixteen. A smart woman would have got the message by now. A decent man would have learned not to make dates he didn't intend to keep.'

She made a careful note on the file in front of her, waited for the excuse. She knew it would be good. He'd had a lot of practice.

'The Chelsea kitchen flooded.'

Yes, that was good, and no doubt true, since all she had to do was pick up a phone and check for herself.

And she wasn't unreasonable. It was a crisis. They happened. All he'd had to do was call her. She wouldn't have been happy, but she'd have understood.

When he didn't continue, didn't offer an apology, she finally looked up. A mistake.

Until now, she'd been protected from her feelings, had believed that to love him in this way was wrong. Inside that shell she'd been able to keep up the pretence that she loathed him. It wasn't just a dress that she'd let fall at her feet, it had been the armour plating with which she'd protected herself. There was more than one way of being naked…

'You want me to use that in the marketing campaign?' she prompted, attempting to regain that lost ground.

'You're angry.'

'Only with myself,' she said, with a dismissive gesture. Before she could resume reading the report in front of her, he caught her hand.

'Please, sweetheart, try to understand.'

She swallowed. His hand was cool, strong, but then he *was* strong. He'd always been the first one to leap in to take care of problems. Always been there when a broad pair of shoulders was needed. She'd seen him taking care of the staff, concerned about their welfare. Knew he'd paid for private treatment for Martin's wife. She couldn't fault his commitment, his kindness. She just wanted a little of that for herself.

'It was lucky I was there. No one seemed to know where to find the cockstop.'

He sounded so sincere, so *reasonable*. But it wasn't reasonable. It was an excuse.

He was the one who'd challenged her over the secrecy of their relationship, implied that she was running scared. But she wasn't the one with the problem. It was him. All night she'd been going over it. Remembering how, when she'd been alone in defending him, declaring herself, he'd been silent. The only time he'd spoken up was for his precious family. Desperate to hold it together, even though, for him, it had always been falling apart..

He never let the business down. Only her. How many times did it have to happen before she got i through her thick skull.

'Bad management, Max.'

That got to him. Hit him where it hurt…

'Walking away to keep a date with you would have made that better? How? The staff carried on, working up to their ankles in water—'

'Bonuses all round for them, no doubt—'

'They earned it! We rely on them every night of the year. They have to be able to rely on me, too!'

Of course they did. She knew that. She even understood. But deep down, she knew it was more than that.

'Then you did what was most important to you. You have nothing to reproach yourself for,' she said.

'Of course I reproach myself. I let you down but it was long past curtain-up before I'd got everything under control. Then I had to go home and get changed.'

On the point of telling him to close the door on the way out, she hesitated. 'Changed?'

His smile was wry. 'I had a clean shirt in the restaurant, but I needed shoes, socks, trousers…'

Without warning she had a mental picture of him, wading into the situation, not caring about his dinner jacket, dress shirt. About her, waiting for him at the theatre. All he would see was the people who worked for him, whom he knew, cared about, struggling to cope, to carry on as if nothing had happened. How could you not love a man like that?

How could you live with him?

Because this was the reality of a relationship with Max.

'I came to the theatre to meet you.' He reached for her hand. 'Waited until everyone had gone.'

'Am I supposed to apologise for not being there?'

He shook his head. 'I'd tried calling you. When you didn't answer, I assumed you'd decided to stay at the theatre. But then, when I came to the flat, you didn't answer your bell, either. And you'd put the deadlock up on the door.'

'You call *before* you stand someone up. Not to apologise afterwards.' Then, relenting, because she couldn't help herself, 'All you had to do was ring me. Two minutes...'

'I was up to my elbows in freezing water.' He took her other hand. 'If I promise that in future I'll let all the restaurants flood to the ceiling while I call you to tell you I'll be late, will you forgive me?'

'You couldn't make that promise. Not with your hand on your heart, Max,' she said as with a sinking heart she realised the truth. That her father had been partly right about him.

Max wasn't like his father—he wouldn't cheat on her with another woman. Bella Lucia was her only rival for his love. It was always there for him...

'And if you did, I wouldn't believe you.'

He had the grace not to argue. Instead he said 'Will you give me another chance?'

'Last night was important, Max. It was special. A new start.'

Max felt her hands slipping from his grasp. Saw real pain dull her lovely eyes. Knowing that he'd done that to her wrenched at him, tore at something buried so deep that he could not admit it, even to himself. And remembering how he'd challenged her about keeping their relationship a secret, he felt shame.

The secrecy had suited him just fine.

Louise wasn't just any woman. If the family knew about them, he'd have to stand up, say the words. Mean them. The way she had, yesterday. He'd listened to her defend him, praise him, tell the world how she felt about him and, like the fool, he'd stood there like a dummy, unable to respond.

Then afterwards, she'd walked with him, told him about James, torn out her heart and placed it, bleeding in his hands. And even though he knew, he understood, he hadn't been able to respond. All he'd done was grudgingly accept her invitation and then let her down.

He'd used Bella Lucia to wreck every relationship he'd ever had before it became too demanding. To drive women who cared for him away. It was an inbuilt flaw, a consequence of his childhood, he knew. A self-fulfilling expectation of abandonment.

This time it was different. No matter what he had to do, from now on Louise would always come first.

He gripped her fingers, refused to let her break contact. 'Give me another chance, Louise.'

'How many do you need?' She sounded brittle, edgy.

'Just one. Truly. Give me one more chance and I'll never let you down again.'

She didn't answer. She didn't believe him.

For a moment he felt like a drowning man. Sinking. Without hope. And then he understood. Like her, he had to strip his feelings bare…

'I want you in my life, Louise.' Not enough. 'I need you.' There was a flicker of something. Like a light coming on… More than that. Like a fire… 'And when I asked you if you would be at the Valentine party, what I really wanted to say was, will you be my date?'

'Your date?'

'My first and only Valentine.' Then, as she smiled. 'Say yes, and I promise you that there will be no tears before bedtime.'

'Tears…?'

'Say the word, Louise, and I promise that on the night I'll be bearing the essential diamond. I love you, Louise.'

Louise's breath caught in her throat. He was really saying he loved her? Was asking her to marry him? For a split second she felt like Cinderella must have done when she tried on the glass slipper.

Then reality crashed in.

'Max…' she warned.

'That's the wrong word.'

'No…'

'Now you're just playing hard to get.' From supplicant to the Max she knew in one easy bound.

She shook her head. 'It's too soon. We need time to get to know one another.'

'We've known one another all our lives, Louise. It's the sex we're catching up on.'

Was it? Really? Could he change, just like that? Unlikely… 'It's madness,' she said.

'Oh, well, thanks.'

'You see?' Another minute and they'd be hurling insults… 'You ask me to marry you…' She paused. 'At least I assume that's what you're doing, although a more ham-fisted, ungracious effort would be impossible to imagine, and already I want to throw something at you.'

And without warning he was smiling. 'Well, that's promising. I've missed our spats.'

'Unbelievable!'

'I swear it's true. I've especially missed them since making up became so much fun.'

'Stop it!'

'You want me to woo you, is that it? Do a PR job on myself. Sell you on the idea?'

'If you had the slightest clue about how to do that,' she informed him, 'you wouldn't need me.'

'Not for your marketing skills, no.' He was

grinning… How dared he be grinning? 'Since we're being brutally honest here, you should know that I'd be happy to keep you around just for your highly imaginative taste in underwear.'

It wasn't a blush searing her cheeks. It was the combination of the winter sunshine striking in through the window and the central heating turned up too high…

'You're not doing a good job of selling me on the idea of marriage, Max.'

'You're not making it easy.'

Louise didn't want to be 'sold'. Or to make it easy for him. He was right, they were having fun, but he was still Max Valentine. The same man who'd left her high and dry more times than a girl with any kind of a life should be able to recall.

Hearing the last bell calling the audience to their seats, being the only person left in the theatre foyer was still painfully fresh.

He'd promised it was the last time, but could he change? When it came to a choice between *Bella Lucia* and her, would he ever put her first?

'There's no such thing as an easy sell,' she told him. 'You need to do your market research.'

'Is that right? For that I need your co-operation Dinner at my place? Nine o'clock.'

She should say no…

And yet… And yet… When he'd held onto her

hands, she'd seen something in his face, something more than the light banter. And when he'd said he loved her, she'd known he was telling the truth.

'Nine o'clock? You're sure you can manage that?'

He crossed his heart. 'You can depend on it.'

Max's apartment was in an ultra modern development overlooking the marina in Chelsea. He had acres of blond-wood open-plan floor-space, a space-age kitchen and simple, minimalist furniture that enveloped her as she sank onto the soft leather sofa.

'Hungry?' he asked.

'Not desperately. My mother came up to town and took me out to lunch.'

'Then we'll leave it for a while. Everything okay? With your mother?'

'Hugs, tears. She wanted to know about us.'

'What did you tell her?'

She grinned. 'As little as I could get away with. She's like Dad. Suspects it will all end in tears.'

'And you?' He handed her a glass of white wine. 'What do you think?'

'I think they're probably right,' she said, taking a sip. Then, 'But I'm here to be sold.'

'Right. Well, round one involves a questionnaire.'

'Oh?'

'The kind of thing that you do,' he said. 'Branding?'

She nodded. 'You need to know what I feel about you so that you can build on your pluses. And round two?'

'That rather depends on how round one goes.'

'Right,' she said, setting her drink on the table, kicking off her boots, tucking a cushion at her back and stretching out on the sofa. 'I'm sitting comfortably. You can begin.'

He lifted her legs, sat down beside her and dropped them across his lap. 'Okay,' he said, absently stroking her feet. 'First question. What three words would you use to describe me?'

'Arrogant,' she said. 'Workaholic. Hot.'

'Arrogant?'

'You don't get to comment on the answers. You collate them, study them, act on the information they give you.'

'Arrogant?' he repeated.

'You don't object to "workaholic" or "hot"?'

'Workaholic is the bad one?'

'I'm not here to do the work for you, Max. You have to study all the results. Ask yourself what's important. What you have to change to get the outcome you want.'

'I see.'

'Two out of three isn't bad,' she said.

'Only if they're the right two.'

'True.' He was, it seemed, learning. 'Shall we

move on? I said I wasn't desperately hungry but I will want to eat tonight.'

'If I was a country which one would I be?'

'Switzerland.'

He frowned. 'Why's that?'

'I refer you to the answer I gave earlier.' Then, 'You're like a Swiss clock; you never stop.'

'I could wind down a little.' She refused to be drawn into a discussion of every answer. That wasn't how it worked. 'A landscape?' he continued.

'Birmingham, Stoke…something industrial.'

'No need to hammer the point. I get the picture. I work too hard.'

'We both work hard, Max. The difference is that you put work first.'

'People rely on me.'

'Delegate.'

'I'm trying, Lou.'

'What would you do if someone phoned from Mayfair, right now, and said the restaurant was on fire?'

'Tell them to call the fire brigade?'

'Liar.' Then, because maybe she was learning something from this, too, 'I'd expect you to go, Max. I'd want to be with you.'

For a moment he seemed lost for words. As if the idea of dealing with a crisis together hadn't occurred to him.

'If I was a time of day?' he said, moving on.

'Six-thirty.'

He smiled at that and she knew he'd got it. Understood that the time she associated with him was that moment when she walked into his office at the end of the day and he stopped whatever he was doing, they had a drink and just talked. Even when he'd been working on the Valentine party, and she'd left him to get on with it, because she knew how important it was. It worked both ways.

'Remember that one, Max,' she said. 'That one's important.'

'A smell?'

Uh-oh, she'd been doing so well until then. In control. Now, without warning, she was plunged into the scent of warm skin, sharp, clean sweat, newly washed hair.

'Shampoo,' she said, quickly.

'And if I was a shampoo, which would it be?'

'Mine.' Her turn to smile. Well, she'd written the questionnaire, she'd known which question was coming next.

'And finally, a car?'

'Anything expensive, fast and reliable.'

'Reliable?'

Never lets you down, she thought. No wonder he'd picked up on that one. What on earth had she been thinking?

'Scratch "reliable",' she said. 'Make that durable.' Then, because he gave her a sharp look that suggested he hadn't missed the subtle difference, 'It goes with the Swiss clock.'

CHAPTER TEN

'MAX…'

Max had stopped stroking her feet and Louise realised that her words had hit home. Maybe there was hope for him and, curling herself up onto her knees, she reached out to him and, playfully ruffling her fingers through his hair, she said, 'Why don't we move on to part two?'

'Part two?' He looked at her. 'Is there any point? You've made it very clear that you think I'm just a work-obsessed—'

She put her fingers over his mouth. 'I told you, Max, the skill is in interpretation. You have to look at *all* the results. It's just as dangerous to concentrate on the words that sting, as it is to grab for the words that confirm what you want to hear. Only then can you act to change things.'

He regarded her with the suspicion of a smile. 'You think?'

'I think,' she assured him. 'Trust me, Max. I'm the expert and it's not over until it's over.'

He shook his head. 'Maybe another time…'

'No.' She didn't want him to think he'd failed. She wanted him to understand what she wanted, needed. That she needed him…

'Part two,' she said, firmly.

'I don't…'

'But I do.' And since she knew what came next, she prompted, 'Which three words would you use to describe your feelings of anticipation about using the Max Valentine product?' she prompted.

'I'm a product?'

'For the purposes of market research. Work with me on this.'

He shrugged, took a breath and, looking straight ahead, as if dreading her answers, he obediently repeated, 'What three words would you use to describe your feelings of anticipation about using the Max Valentine product?'

'Urgency,' she offered. 'Excitement. Impatience…'

He glanced at her, the beginning of a smile tugging at his lips. 'Impatience?'

Suiting the deed to the word, Louise locked her arms around his neck and swung herself over to sit astride his lap.

'Which three words,' she said as she began to unbutton his shirt, 'would you use to describe your feelings during the use of this product?'

'Which three words…' he began. She leaned into

him, stopping the words with her mouth, and when she'd got his full attention and he was kissing her back she moved on to trail her lips over his throat, across his chest. Then, as she began to unfasten his belt…

'Desire. Passion. Heat…'

It was much later when, her eyes closed, her voice dreamy, soft with fulfilment, she said, 'Which three words would you use to describe how you feel after using this product…?'

'Shattered,' Max said, before she could answer her own question. 'Sated.' He kissed her. 'Complete.'

'Good answers,' she murmured.

'You give good questions,' Max said, touching her face, stroking back her hair. 'I loved your version of part two.' Then, 'Can we try mine now?'

She opened her eyes. 'You had a different version?'

'My part two consisted of me going down on one knee and asking you to marry me. When I failed part one—'

'This isn't an exam,' she said, quickly, cutting him off. She was still sure that it was too soon. He hadn't failed, but she was certain that he needed time to think about this. Or maybe she was the one fooling herself. Maybe she was the one who needed time… 'There are no right or wrong answers.'

'I know. It's all in the interpretation, but it's pretty

clear that you think I'm work obsessed. That I put the restaurant before everything else.'

'I don't care about everything else. My problem is that you put the restaurant before me. You always have.'

On the point of denying it, he nodded. 'You're right. I should have called you last night.'

'No. You should have been there. Last night was important to me. Important for us. I think that scared you.'

'No!' Then, 'Maybe, just a bit, but there was a crisis. I didn't spend time considering options, I just did what needed to be done. You know how it gets.'

She knew. And, despite everything, she did understand. But she wasn't letting him off the hook on this one. He needed to understand her point of view.

'That was the manager's job. You shouldn't have even been there, Max. Your role is to look at the bigger picture now. You have to trust your staff to deal with the day to day problems.' She shook her head. 'Failing that, you take time to make a call. Look, I know how it is. I've waited tables at functions when staff haven't turned in for a PR do but my mother taught me to use a phone when I was very small. To call home when I was going to be late. To call someone when you can't make a date.'

'I'm from a broken home,' he said.

'That's it, Max.' They'd got to the heart of the problem. Finally. 'You want the whole-heart relationship, but you're afraid of the commitment. Afraid of being hurt.'

'You're right.' He closed his eyes. 'You think I never put you before work, but let me tell you that I've spent all day thinking about us. Thinking about me. How I am. I won't ever do that to you again. I promise.'

'Promises and pie crusts,' she said. 'Made to be broken.'

'Not this time. You have my word.' Then, 'You do believe me?'

'I believe that you mean it now. Tomorrow... The day after...'

'No. You have to believe. It's more than that. I can't lose you.' He reached for her, wrapped his arms around her. 'Not now I've found you. I want us to be together always. I want you to be my wife, Louise.'

A lump rose to her throat, so that she couldn't speak. It was like all the Christmases, birthdays, Valentine's Days, rolled into one. Every dream coming true.

And still she hesitated.

She knew that at that moment Max would have promised her anything. Deep down inside her, though, there was still that small nagging doubt. That he meant everything he said, she was certain. Whether he still understood what that meant, she wasn't totally certain. Wasn't convinced that it was a risk she should take.

But then she'd learned from experience that safety wasn't enough, either. James had been a safe bet, 'a banker', the kind of husband any woman would be fortunate to have.

Max, on the other hand, was always going to be a gamble. But when life without him meant putting her heart into permanent cold storage…

'Why don't you save it until the fourteenth, Max?'

'The fourteenth?'

'Valentine's Day. We have a date, or have you forgotten already?'

'Actually, I don't remember you saying yes to that.'

'I didn't. I'm saying it now. Turn up with the ring in your pocket, do your stuff then and we'll make an announcement.' Her flippant tone gave nothing away of the tangle of emotions in her heart.

'You want me to go down on one knee in front of everyone?'

'Would you do that for me?'

He hesitated for barely a second. 'Anything.'

'I'm the only one you have to convince, Max,' she said, then leaned across and kissed him. 'Make it a solitaire. Not too big. I don't want it to look as if it came out of a Christmas cracker. Now, can we eat?'

* * *

Everyone worked on Valentine's Day. Even John and Robert were pressed into service at the Mayfair restaurant, working together, a pair of world-class experts in smoothing out wrinkles, keeping diners whose tables were delayed from getting fractious.

Max was at the Knightsbridge restaurant. Lavish, contemporary, it was a favourite with the social elite as well as the aristocracy of the theatre.

Louise was playing hostess at the Chelsea restaurant, a popular haunt with the livelier celebrities who arrived trailing a crowd of paparazzi. She knew them all and would be at her best there, Max knew, and, as the original restaurant, it was traditionally where they held the huge after-hours party where everyone, all the staff, all the family, gathered to celebrate the year.

This year, as their diamond anniversary, was extra special in more ways than one. Max patted his jacket where the ring he was going to give Louise—a solitaire, a single carat, he wanted her to know that he'd been listening—was tucked into his ticket pocket, along with the safety pin she'd given him.

When he'd emptied his pockets on his return from Meridia, it had been there among his change and keys. Such a small thing and yet it had signalled a change in their relationship: a move from war to peace. A symbol, a link that somehow held them together, and since the night when he'd told her he loved her, asked her to marry him, he'd taken to carrying it with him.

He hoped to get away some time in the evening. He'd arranged for a bottle of Krug to be waiting in the tiny office and, with the door firmly closed, he'd make a proper job of his proposal. He'd seen the flicker of uncertainty in her eyes. A momentary shadow of doubt. He had to convince her, once and for all, that without her Bella Lucia meant nothing to him. It was true. He'd looked into the abyss, the dark emptiness of life without her, and he knew it was true. She would always come first.

He glanced at his watch. Ten o'clock. A quick look around. Everything was humming. No problems. He could slip away now, be back before…

'Mr Valentine—' He turned at the hushed urgency in the *maître d*'s voice '—we've got a bit of a problem.'

No. Not tonight…

'I'm just leaving, Jane. See Stephanie.' Nothing, no one, would stop him from putting Louise first tonight.

'It's not…please…'

She looked as if she might faint. 'Steady, now. What is it? What's the matter?'

'Table five. Charles Prideaux. The actor?' she added, in case he didn't know. 'He's not well.'

'What's the matter with him?'

She pulled herself together. 'He's clammy, no colour, complaining of indigestion.'

'Classic indications of a heart attack. Call an ambulance,' he said, turning away.

'No! He won't allow it. He doesn't want to attract attention. He seems more concerned about his wife finding out he's here with some young actress when he was supposed to be at a business meeting than whether he's about to die.'

'The two may not be mutually exclusive.' But not in one of his restaurants. 'Where is he?'

'One of the other diners found him in difficulties in the loo and called a waiter. We've put him in the office.'

Who's with him?'

'No one. He wouldn't let me get anyone else even though I'm not a first aider. He said I could only get you.'

'Hell, he shouldn't be left alone.' Whether he liked it or not, Max was involved. 'OK, Jane, it's not your fault—you've done well, considering the circumstances. I'll take it from here. Can he walk?'

'With help.'

He looked at his watch. It would take half an hour, no more. 'Get him back to him now and take him out through the rear. I'll drive him to the nearest A and E.'

* * *

Louise took a tray of coffee out to the paparazzi wanting to be the first with photos of newly acquired diamonds. It was cold out there and, despite their bad press, she understood they were just doing a job like everyone else. And their presence meant the restaurant was a favourite with A-list celebrities.

If she hoped to catch a sight of an eager Max arriving early she wasn't admitting it, not even to herself.

So far the day had gone well.

Among a very impressive, but ultimately clichéd, number of red roses, it was the elegant basket of lilies of the valley that had been delivered to her desk from a fashionable florist—sweetly scented, pure as a child's promise—that stood out.

There was no name on the card—unlike the roses, which had been mostly from party organisers, people who wanted to be in her good books and used the play on her name as an excuse to remind her of their existence. There were just four words.

"For my first Valentine."

Gemma had been seriously impressed and it took a lot to impress her.

'Any scoops, Louise?' Glad of the distraction, she turned to the photographer. 'Anything we can phone in to the news desk?'

Several sets of tantrums, a lot of tears—not all of

them from the women—but nothing unusual on an occasion so invested with emotion.

'You know the secrets of the dining table are sacrosanct, Pete.'

'What about you?' he asked, changing tack. 'Rumour has it that Max was seen coming out of Garrard's earlier in the week.'

Garrard's? A visit to the royal jeweller's suggested he'd taken her words to heart, but she kept the cool smile in place, said, 'Now you're just fishing.'

'And I think I just got a nibble.' He grinned. 'You didn't deny it, you just changed the subject. As good as an admission from someone in PR.'

'Louise!' She turned as one of the waitresses put her head around the door. 'You're wanted.'

Max…

'Table three. He says he wants to thank you for introducing him to the girl he's with. At some party? They've just got engaged.'

'Oh, right. I'm coming,' she said, throwing a quick glance in the direction of Sloane Square. Stupid. He hadn't said he'd be early; it was just that she'd seen the champagne, was aware of an undercurrent of excitement, of furtive glances in her direction.

Max would be here. He'd promised.

He was busy. They were all busy, but he wouldn't let her down. Wouldn't let Bella Lucia down. This was BL's party as much as theirs…

Max hadn't banked on being saddled with the girlfriend.

'I have to go with him,' she said. 'He might die.'

There was no time to argue and he bundled her in, making the hospital in record time, but that wasn't the end of it.

'Call my wife,' Prideaux begged. 'Tell her where I am.' Then, 'Make sure Gina gets home safely.'

The words said one thing, his eyes said another, sending out a desperate plea to get the girl out of the way before his wife turned up.

Easier said than done. Gina was having hysterics and convinced her lover was about to die, was vowing never to leave his side.

It took him and two nurses to prise her from Charles Prideaux's side, get her out of the treatment room. At which point she flung herself, sobbing, into his arms.

As he comforted her, absently reassured her, he stared at the clock, ticking remorselessly round to eleven. Louise wouldn't expect him before half past.

There was time.

It took patience, endless tact, to get Gina calmed

down, to explain that the hospital had called Charles's wife, that she would have to leave.

When he thought that she'd finally got it, that he could put her in a taxi and go to Louise, she sat down in the waiting room in the manner of a woman who was not to be shifted.

'Let her come. She needs to know about us. That Charles is going to leave her.'

He didn't care about her. Or Charles Prideaux.

He did care about some innocent woman who'd walk into this. He knew what that was like. He'd seen it happen three times. Seen the fallout. The agony. And not just for the women involved, but for the children.

'Gina, this isn't the moment. Charles isn't in any state to cope with this kind of emotional upheaval. He needs to be calm right now if he's going to make any kind of recovery.'

The tears started again, but she didn't resist as he steered her through the main doors. 'Where do you live?' he asked.

'Battersea.'

He took a deep breath. 'I'll take you home.'

'It's okay, Max. You've done enough. I'll get a taxi.'

He would have liked nothing better, but he didn't trust her. She was an actress looking for an easy route to stardom. Why else would she be out with a married man twice her age? There was no doubt in his mind that the minute he left her, she'd be back inside, waiting for Mrs Prideaux to arrive. Act out her big scene. She'd quite possibly call the tabloids to make sure she got maximum publicity, too.

'Charles asked me to make sure you get home safely, Gina,' he said. 'And that's what I'm going to do.'

She swore, then. Proving he'd been right. Ignoring her rage, he opened the car door and after a moment she got in.

He took a breath. A result. Now all he had to do was call Louise, put her in the picture. Even as he reached for his cell phone he realised he didn't have it with him. They were forbidden in the restaurant and he always made a habit of putting his away in the office.

Half an hour. He'd be there.

Max hadn't come.

She had watched the staff from the Chelsea restaurant arrive, but he wasn't with them. She'd waited for someone to pass on a message, some explanation of the hold-up. She had imagined car accidents, every kind of disaster.

Even his father had been concerned. Max was, after all, the host this year. This was his party. His celebration. His role to thank everyone for their hard work.

She'd heard Robert ask Stephanie, her half-brother Daniel's wife and the Knightbridge restaurant's manager, where he was. But she'd shaken her head.

'He left at about ten. Everything was running smoothly. I assumed he was coming here.'

Louise was standing outside in the small court-yard in front of the restaurant where, in the summer, people liked to eat alfresco. It was empty now, too cold to tempt anyone outside. She stood listening to his cell phone ring. The voicemail click in, his familiar voice asking her to leave a message, that he would get back to her.

He wouldn't.

He'd tried. She understood that. Knew that if he'd ever loved anyone, he'd loved her. But it hadn't been enough. He still couldn't break free, make that leap to commitment. Maybe it had been wrong of her to expect it. He was who he was. The result of his upbringing, just as she was. Nurture over nature. She'd gone into this with her eyes open, expecting, wanting, no more than a brief, exciting affair.

She'd had that.

And it had been exciting. Wonderful. And it was over.

She turned as the door opened behind her. Her parents were leaving.

'Louise?' her mother said. 'What are you doing out here on your own?'

'I just needed some air. Are you leaving?'

'It's been a long evening. I don't want your father overdoing things.'

'I suspect he's made of sterner stuff than you give him credit for,' Louise said, with a smile she dredged up from the soles of her designer shoes.

'Any sign of Max?' her father asked, glancing at the phone in her hand.

She snapped it shut. 'No.' Then she shivered despite the warmth of her coat. 'To be honest I'm about done here.'

Done with Max. Done with Bella Lucia. Done with the icy damp of a London winter.

'Do you want a lift home?'

'It'll take you out of your way.'

'No problem.' He ushered her into the back seat next to her mother, then, having given the driver her address, climbed in next to her.

Neither of them mentioned Max again. Instead as they headed towards Kensington her mother chatted brightly about a holiday they were planning, doing their best to distract her so that she didn't have to do more than drop in the occasional "umm". Pretty much all her aching throat could manage.

'Louise?' Her mother took her hand, stopped her before she left the car. 'Are you going to be all right?'

'Fine,' she said, pulling herself together, pasting

on a smile, hugging them both, fiercely. 'Fine. I'll call you tomorrow.'

The red light on her answering machine was winking at her as she let herself in. She switched it on and it informed her that she had 'one new message'.

'Lou? It's Cal. I'll be in London tomorrow—' She switched it off. He might be, but she wouldn't.

'Have you seen Louise?'

He knew he was in trouble.

It had taken hours to get rid of Gina. She'd had him driving round in circles, taking out her anger, her disappointment, on him. He would have appealed to her better nature, assuming that she had one, but he doubted that a plea to smooth his own path to married bliss would have moved her to pity.

He'd gritted his teeth, telling himself that Louise would have heard what had happened, understand why he had been held up. That he hadn't stood her up for Bella Lucia.

The party seemed to be in its final stages. Slow music, couples wrapped in each other's arms. His father was sitting in the bar, a glass of malt in his hand. Wife number four, Bev, was vainly trying to get him to leave.

'Lost her, have you? Careless that. But you're a Valentine. We're made that way.'

'She's gone, Max,' Bev told him. 'I put my head out of the door for some fresh air and saw her leaving with John and Ivy.'

'Uh-oh. You are in serious trouble,' his father said, pointing at him with the glass, which was clearly not his first.

'More serious than you know.'

'You were supposed to make a speech, too. Or had you forgotten that? Thanks for all the hard work. Great year. Expansion…'

And the rest. The extra bit about Louise Valentine making him the happiest man alive.

He'd got that wrong, too.

Again.

If he hadn't bottled out of the gala, tonight wouldn't have been such a huge, make-or-break deal.

He hadn't been putting nearly enough effort into making her the happiest woman…

It was very late when he pulled up in front of Louise's apartment, but he couldn't let her go to sleep believing that he'd let her down. He had to explain. And when he looked up he could see that there were lights on. Despite his relief that she was still awake, he suspected that was not a good sign. It was the same intuition that warned him not to use the key she'd given him, but ring the bell.

'Yes?'

'I need to talk to you, Louise. To explain.'

He'd anticipated resistance, but she buzzed him up without comment. She was still wearing her evening clothes. A dark red figure skimming dress that was slit to the thigh.

'You look lovely,' he said, moving to kiss her.

'Thank you,' she said, turning away before he could touch her.

He'd expected a rocket. Missiles. Fire.

Her cold politeness was much, much worse. He prayed that she was simply thinking of her neighbours...

'Look, I'm sorry I didn't get to the party before you left.' She waited, her back to him, very still. 'I had to take a guest to the hospital. Charles Prideaux, the actor.'

'Really? I hope he gave you his autograph.'

'Surely someone told you?'

'No one knew where you were.' She spun round to face him. 'Forget me for a moment, Max. That we had a date. That you were going to turn up with the ring and we were going to announce our engagement. You let down your staff, too.'

'Lou...' He hadn't anticipated this kind of reaction. Louise, calm, was a whole new experience and he didn't know how to get through to her. 'I had to take the man's girlfriend home. Before his wife arrived. She was difficult.'

'That was not your problem, Max.'

'Yes, dammit, it was. She was going to stay and make a scene. Confront his wife.'

'And you thought it was your duty to protect the man from the fallout of his infidelity?'

'Protect his wife.'

'Of course. My mistake.'

'You do understand, then?'

'Yes, Max. I understand.'

She didn't sound as if she did. If she'd understood, she'd have put her arms around him and held him and made the whole hideous episode go away.

Louise looked at him, confused, a little angry, and thought her heart might just break.

When she'd heard the car draw up outside, had looked out and seen it was Max, her first thought had been to ignore him. She'd used the deadlock on the door so he couldn't get in. Then he'd rung the doorbell, taking her by surprise, and she'd known that wouldn't do.

She owed herself more than that. She needed to face him. Put an end to this once and for all. She'd buzzed him up and then slipped out of her wrap and back into her dress. Stepped into shoes that brought her nearly to his height. Full body armour.

She'd wanted him to see that after tonight there was nothing he could do or say that could provoke her into anger, or reduce her to tears. But even then, some little part of her heart had hoped that he'd find a way to touch her. Bring her back to life.

But she couldn't allow it.

Tonight he'd not only stood her up, but he'd stood up Bella Lucia to save some sham of marriage. Still trying, in his head, to protect his mother from his father's infidelity. To save himself from the fallout.

And he had no idea what he'd done. He thought he could brush it aside, that all he had to do was turn up, explain and everything would be all right.

'Is that it?' she asked.

'You want me to go?'

He sounded surprised.

'You've apologised, explained. What else did you have in mind?'

'Don't be like this, Louise. It was a genuine emergency.'

'You should have called an ambulance.'

'Believe me, I wish I had.' Then, 'I have the ring…' He reached into his ticket pocket, produced a perfect diamond solitaire.

'So it's true. You did find time to visit Garrard's?' She took the ring from him before he did anything as hideous as taking her hand and placing it on her finger.

He frowned. 'How did you know that?'

'One of the photographers outside the restaurant said you'd been seen there.' She moved it so that the diamond flashed fire, burning her with its brilli ance. 'Be prepared to read about it in the *Courier's* Diary column tomorrow.'

She took one last look at it, then handed it back. 'You don't like it?'

'It's quite lovely, Max.' But too late. 'Unfortunately if you married me you'd be committing bigamy. You're already married to Bella Lucia.'

'That's ridiculous!'

'Is it? Really?' She considered trying to explain. That she wasn't turning him down just for herself, but for him, too. That forcing him to put her first was hurting him as much as always coming a poor second was hurting her. They were bad for each other. But it was too late. She was too tired. And he wouldn't believe her anyway. Better to keep it simple… 'You did understand what I said on the last occasion you stood me up? You do recall asking for one last chance?'

'Yes, but…'

'But?' She shook her head. 'Don't bother to answer that, Max. There is no "us".'

'If you'd been there…' he said, a little desperately. Then, angry at being backed into a corner, 'I don't know what you expect—'

'I expect nothing from a man who would put business before life.' Her throat was beginning to ache. The words were becoming harder. 'Of a man who is incapable of doing anything else.'

It was why she hadn't leapt in with an eager 'yes' the instant he'd asked her to marry him, she understood that now. Some inner sense of self-preservation had come to her rescue. The small, still voice of common sense telling her that, no matter what he said, he could never change. That she would always be waiting for him to turn up. To a party, their marriage, the rest of their lives.

If she'd made a promise to him nothing short of an act of God would have stopped her from delivering on it, but there was no point in telling him that. All that remained now was pride. The need to walk away with her head high.

'What we had was great while it lasted, Max, but if we're honest it was just sex. Steamy, memorable sex, but nothing more than the gratification of old desires.' The casually dismissive words seemed to be coming from someone else. 'Curiosity satisfied, ghosts laid,' she said. 'Now, we can both move on.'

'No! I don't want to move on. I love you!'

'Need, desire…'

Love was something else. Something more. I was because she loved him that she couldn't stay with him. Knowing that each time he let her down he'd feel more guilt…

Another minute, she begged, enough strength for just one more minute…

She hadn't needed a ring, or even for him to say

the words. The words meant nothing. 'I love you' was in what you did, the way you treated someone.

This was how James must have felt, she realised. Maybe she deserved this numbing blow to her heart that, for the moment, left her beyond feeling. She should be grateful for that reprieve, however short. The pain would come soon enough, but it was a familiar heartache. She'd lived with it before. Through all the years when he was out of reach. She could live with it again. For the moment all she asked was the strength to finish it without falling apart and she crossed to the door, opened it, a silent invitation to leave.

For a long moment Max didn't move. He just looked at her with the bewildered expression of a child who'd been shouted at and didn't know why.

He just didn't get it. Never would...

'Please...' she said.

It sounded too much like a plea, too weak and in two strides he was beside her. For a moment she thought he was going to seize her, kiss her as he had before when she'd been on the point of walking away. But this time he just stood there, looking at her as if he was imprinting her image on his brain. Or maybe that was her, taking one last look...

'I'll see you tomorrow?' he asked, finally. 'At six-thirty?'

Business as usual? Was he serious?

It was too much…

'You will be there?' he pressed when she didn't answer.

She shook her head, but he didn't take it as a refusal, only as an admission that she didn't know.

'You're exhausted,' he said. 'We'll talk about this tomorrow.' And then he walked through the door she was not so much holding open as clinging to, down the stairs, out of her apartment. Out of her life.

It was all she could do not to call him back but she hung onto her sanity just long enough to hear the street door close. To close and lock her own front door.

It was only when she heard his car start, pull away from the kerb, that all the bottled up emotion shattered and she picked up her answering machine and hurled it at the wall, where it broke in a dozen pieces, along with her heart.

CHAPTER ELEVEN

MAX left because she'd given him no other option. Louise had somehow managed to blank herself off from him, put herself some place far beyond the flare-up of temper that would have worked for him. He could have used her passion to break her down, bring her into his arms, but she'd put up a wall of ice to keep him out.

That in her own living room at close to two o'clock in the morning, she'd been wearing high heels, a dress he knew she'd have discarded for the comfort of her wrap the minute she'd got home, told him that it was deliberate. That she was playing a part.

The fact that she was still awake, clearly hadn't even thought about bed, bothered him more. She hadn't removed her make-up, and her hair was pinned up in that sexy way that suggested all it would take was one pin to bring it all tumbling down in his hands.

It all suggested that sleep had been the last thing on her mind. That she had more important things to do…

He pulled over, turned in his seat to look back. Her light was still on and for a moment he was tempted to go back, do anything, promise anything…

No.

She'd made it clear that she thought his promises were meaningless, and she was right. He'd been making promises to her all his life and then letting her down.

He needed to think about that. Really think about it before he could go back, attempt to change her mind, convince her that he wanted to be with her for the rest of his life. He had to ask himself not what he wanted, but what Louise wanted from their relationship. And why he wasn't giving it to her.

She'd told him all he needed to know, but, convinced that the proposal was nothing more than formality, he hadn't bothered to use the information. Analyse it. Hadn't listened to what she'd been telling him.

What three words would you use to describe yourself…?

Driven. Dumb. Dumped.

Louise went back to her packing. Concentrating on folding, packing. It took a while. She'd need suits as well as holiday clothes for this trip.

The last time she'd gone to Melbourne, she'd been running away from one family, searching for a new one. This time was different. This time she was re-claiming her life from a crippling obsession that had held her in its thrall since childhood hero-worship of Max had changed into something out of reach. Ultimately destructive.

She should have had a husband, children of her own by now, but there was no going back.

She didn't have a family of her own and it seemed unlikely that she ever would have. But she did have a thriving business and a talented assistant whom she was ready to make a partner.

Gemma could bring in a junior, continue to run the London office. She, in the meantime, would concentrate on expanding her own business. Stop scanning the horizon for something, someone, who would never be there.

Her phone began to ring. It was the airline con-firming her seat on the evening flight out of London Heathrow.

That was something her contact at the diary page of the *Courier* would be interested in, she thought. An unmistakable message that even Max would understand.

And a kindness. In his anger, he'd blame her. She didn't want him to feel guilty. He was how he was. He couldn't help it.

She'd call Gemma first thing, catch her before she left for the office and brief her about everything that had to be done. She'd better call Patsy, too, in case there was anything she wanted to send to Jodie. Then she'd spend the day with her parents out at Richmond Hill before going straight on to the airport.

Max...

He'd asked her if she planned keeping their six-thirty date. Well, it was just business, so it didn't matter if it was Gemma who delivered the completed marketing plan which was, even now, sitting on her desk waiting to be delivered.

At six-thirty, she'd be unfastening her seat belt. Settling in for the long flight east.

She replaced the receiver, then bent to pick up the pieces of broken answering machine that were spread all over the carpet.

Under one of the larger pieces, she found a tiny gold safety pin. She looked at it for a moment, sitting back on her heels, wondering how on earth it could have got there. Even if she'd dropped it, and she couldn't imagine how since the only pins she had were kept in the carryall she used for work or travelling, her cleaner had been in yesterday morning and she wouldn't have missed it.

She reached out a finger and touched it, remembering the moment when she'd given one exactly like it to Max. How he'd taken it. Put it in his ticket pocket, next to his heart.

It had been a special moment. A moment when anything might have happened. When it *had* happened.

No regrets.

She'd got what she'd wanted. If it hadn't worked out quite the way she'd expected, if she hadn't managed to get Max out of her system, she still had more than she'd ever dreamed possible. She'd dared to risk everything and, even if she didn't have Max, she had somehow reclaimed her life. No more deep freeze…

She picked up the pin, placed it on the table beside the broken bits of answering machine, then frowned as she remembered the moment Max had pulled that damned ring out of the same pocket.

No. It couldn't be. He'd been wearing a dinner jacket tonight.

For it to be the same pin, he'd have had to move it from suit to suit along with the rest of the contents of his pockets that he carried with him, always.

'It doesn't mean anything,' she whispered. 'It's just habit…'

But even as she said the words a tear welled up, fell. Soaked into the carpet.

Max hadn't slept. He'd spent the night thinking. About Louise. About himself. About the bleakness of a future in which she wasn't there at the start and end of every day.

Shining a light into every corner of their relationship, exposing feelings that he'd always refused to acknowledge, finally understanding a pattern of behaviour that had ended in that scene last night.

Searching for some way to show her that, despite everything he'd done, he was serious. That she was more important to him than a hundred restaurants. That he loved her…

He woke, groggy, just before ten, still in the armchair, an idea, half formed, struggling to the surface. He showered, shaved. Resisted the urge to go straight to her office and tell her what he was going to do.

Six-thirty. That was their time.

It would give him time to put his plan into action so that she'd understand that it wasn't some empty promise.

She had to understand.

It was his secretary, bringing in the mail, who looked doubtful. She listened to him telling the company lawyer to set the wheels in motion, insisting that it be done in time for his daily meeting with Louise, then, when he rang off, said, 'Are you expecting Louise this evening?'

'Has she called to say she can't make it?'

'No, but…'

'But what?'

She went and fetched the early edition of the *Courier*, folded it back at the diary page.

In between a torn heart, one enclosing a photograph of Louise, one of himself, was the headline:

"NO DIAMONDS FOR THESE VALENTINES...

Expectations were high of an announcement that Max Valentine had popped the question to his latest squeeze, Louise Valentine, at the Bella Lucia Diamond Jubilee party last night. Max, who has been working with Louise on the expansion of the restaurant group, with new premises in Qu'Arim and Meridia already well in hand, was spotted recently in the Queen's jewellers, Garrard's, investing heavily in a girl's best friend.

Max, however, wasn't at the party and I have it on good authority that London's favourite PR consultant has already booked her business class ticket and is at this very moment packing her bags, preparing to hotfoot it to Australia, eager to expand her own expire.

He didn't stop to question the veracity of this statement. It rang too horribly true. Instead he raced to her apartment, grabbed the front door as someone was leaving and raced upstairs, hammered on the door to her apartment.

It was opened by Cal Jameson.

'Max,' he said. 'Louise said to expect you.'

'She's here?' Relief flooded through him. 'I have to see her, tell her…'

'She was leaving as I arrived,' Cal said. 'Gave me a key, told me to make myself at home. I'm staying for a week this time—'

'Where is she?' he demanded, cutting him short. He wasn't interested in Cal Jameson's plans. Only in finding Louise.

'I couldn't say *exactly*. Somewhere between here and Melbourne. That's in Australia,' the younger man added helpfully.

'She's gone? Already?' Max clawed back his hair. 'She can't have. What about work? Her parents?'

'Damm it, Max. You've got it bad. You need a drink—'

'I don't want a drink. I just want—'

'Louise. I know, mate. I know. You'd better come in.'

Louise gripped the arms of the seat, hating the moment of take-off. Hating the moment when the huge jet banked over London. Letting out a sigh of relief as the ping of the seat-belt warning light went off.

A stewardess offered her a drink, but she shook her head. No alcohol, minimum food, lots of water

And sleep. She needed sleep. At least the unexpected upgrade from club to first class gave her all the stretch room she needed.

She even had an empty seat beside her.

No one to disturb her while she laid out her plans for expansion into Australia, she congratulated herself. No one to disturb her, ever again.

It couldn't be more perfect, she told herself as she bent to retrieve her laptop at her feet.

Then someone took the seat beside her.

She glanced sideways at her new companion, nodding distantly, not making eye contact — the last thing she wanted was a chatty travelling companion—then did the fastest double take in history.

'Max!' His name was expelled on what felt like the last breath in her body. Then, 'What are you doing here?'

'It's six-thirty,' he said. 'We always meet at this time of day.'

'But Gemma was going to—'

'Stand in for you? While I'm sure she's a perfectly capable young woman, that wasn't the deal we made. And as I'm sure you'll recall, Louise, I paid in advance.'

She gasped. 'I can't believe you just said that.'

'Of course you can. You can believe anything of me. The fact that you'd get on an aircraft and run away to the other side of the world to avoid me proves it.' He opened his briefcase, took out a thick envelope. 'Not that I don't appreciate it,' he said. 'It has given me an opportunity to demonstrate just how serious I am when I tell you that I'll never stand you up again.'

'I'm not running away!' she said, fiercely. 'This has nothing to do with you, Max. This is about me. I've spent my whole life wanting something just out of reach. It's time to grow up, move on, live the life I've got, not the one I dreamed…'

She applied the brake to her mouth, but not soon enough.

'Not the life you dreamed of?' he asked, gently.

'Not all dreams are good dreams, Max.'

'No. And not all mistakes are bad.' He leaned back, closed his eyes momentarily. 'Not that last night was a mistake. I did what I thought was the right thing, Louise. I can't change who I am.'

'I know. I understand…'

'It was all the other times that I got it wrong. But maybe not entirely wrong.'

Louise swallowed. 'No?'

Oh, that hurt. For the last sixteen sleep-deprived hours, she'd been too numb for the pain to bite, but suddenly, hearing Max say that one word brought her whole body to agonising life and she had to bite back the cry of pain.

'No,' he repeated, then rolled his head to look at

her. 'How else would I have known how it would feel to lose you? How much it would hurt?'

No, no, no... 'Please, Max, don't do this.'

'I have to. I have to explain. If, when I've done, you don't want me here, I'll move to another seat. Go away. Never bother you again.'

That wasn't what she wanted to hear, either, but she took in a deep breath, let it out. Nodded.

'I spent most of the night thinking about us. About how, all my life, I've been pushing you away. Not just the surface stuff, avoiding each other, making sarcastic comments about the boys, the men who trailed after you like puppies. Deeper than that.'

'I didn't know there was anything deeper,' Louise said. Then shook her head. It was so easy to fall into the habits of a lifetime. Dangerous. Sniping led to anger and anger led to passion. And after passion there was only pain...

'I thought about the night I was supposed to take you to your school prom,' Max said, not rising to it. 'We were short-staffed, I didn't lie about that, but if I'd said to Dad that I had to go, reminded him that Uncle John had asked me to be your escort, he'd have found someone to cover.'

'You were more interested in the business even then, Max.'

'No. The truth is that your father had drafted me in as a safe pair of hands, someone he could rely on not to forget himself with "his little princess", was the way he put it. I knew just how you'd look. Sweet, innocent, in a demure frock but with that look in your eyes that said everything. A look I'd have to resist or burn in hell.'

'You were so wrong about that.'

'Wrong?'

'Anything but sweet and innocent. I had a killer dress stashed away in my bag and I had designs on you. You were right to run scared.'

'Really?' A ghost of a smile lit up eyes that were grey with tiredness. 'Uncle John nearly scalped me for standing you up. What he'd have done if he'd even suspected…'

'It didn't happen.' She found an answering smile from somewhere. 'I suppose I should thank you for saving me from myself.'

'I haven't finished, yet. There was the time you were flying to Italy. A year older, you were learning to hide your feelings, but I didn't want you to go. I knew those Italian men would be all over you. That they could have what I wanted.' He dragged his hand over his face. 'When you came back, I could see…'

'What could you see, Max?'

'One look was all it took. One look and I knew that you'd taken that step away from me. I thought something inside me had died.'

'Only thought?'

'When you dropped that slinky dress at your feet,' he said, with a grin, 'I realised it had only been wounded.'

'His name was Roberto,' she told him, by way of punishment. 'Six-foot two, short dark hair, blue eyes.' She shook her head, realising, too late, that she wasn't punishing him, but herself. 'I knew by then that I couldn't have you. Mustn't want you. He was the nearest I could get.' Then, desperate to put that behind her, 'This is ancient history, Max.'

'But don't you see, Lou? It established a pattern. Last week's kitchen flood was just the latest in a long line of similar excuses.'

'But we were together.'

'Were we? Hiding away as if we were ashamed of our feelings?' She waited. 'This was different, Louise. You'd asked me out on a date and it wasn't like dinner with Patsy and Derek—something that could be brushed off as a family thing. It would have been just the two of us at a gala where we'd be recognised by half the audience. You were ready to make that statement, say to the world we're a couple, while my sub-conscious was still programmed to sabotage anything that seemed like a relationship. That was anything more than sex.'

'Is that supposed to be some kind of excuse?'

'Yes. No… I'm just trying to explain that this is what I've been doing all my life. Running away from you. Unable to commit·to anyone else. Telling myself that love is fool's gold, no more than a meaningless convention to lend the lustre of respectability to baser desires. A lesson I learned at my father's knee.'

'So?'

'So last night wasn't like that. I was frantic. I couldn't leave that stupid girl. I didn't have my cell phone to call you. But I was sure someone would have told you what happened. I only learned today that Jane, the one person who knew the whole story, had been too shaken up by the incident to come to the party.'

'Oh.'

'Last night I tried to help someone in trouble. You need to know that I'll always do that, even when it isn't convenient. Even when it's downright inconvenient. Just as you need to know that I will always put you before Bella Lucia. I meant what I said the other night. I love you.'

He produced the ring from his pocket, held it in the palm of his hand. 'You can stop looking at the horizon, Lou. I'm here. This is yours. Along with my heart.'

When she didn't take it, he closed his hand around it, took a document from the envelope, tucked the ring inside.

'Maybe this will convince you I'm serious.'

'What is this?'

'A partnership in Bella Lucia.'

'A partnership?' For a moment she didn't know whether to laugh or cry. Did he really think that would make a difference?

'An equal partnership. Take it, Louise, be my partner in everything, or I'm going to quit the business.'

What? 'You can't do that, Max. It's your life.'

'No, you are my life. And without you...' she waited '...what would be the point?'

Her words. What she'd said to him. When he'd asked her why she'd stopped dating. What would have been the point?

'What, my love? You think I don't know? You think I haven't been there? One woman in my arms and another so deeply ingrained in every cell that nothing I do can drive out the thought of her?'

She searched his face, saw the truth. That he had reached deep, found something within himself. Surrendered himself in a way that she'd never thought possible.

Not that he wouldn't get distracted, drawn towards some new scheme and forget everything else for a moment. But it would be the normal distractions that everyone lived with. He would never be running from her again.

'What would you do?' she asked. 'If I said no?'

'Become a beach bum,' he said. 'Take up surfing. Cal Jameson promised to give me lessons.'

'Cal?'

'He was the one who found out what plane you were on. Organised the upgrade so that I could sit beside you.'

'You mean it wasn't just luck? That you paid…' She frowned. 'So where were you? Why did you wait until we'd taken off?'

'Our date was for six-thirty. It was the one time I knew you'd be thinking of me.'

'Oh.'

'And I wanted to be sure you couldn't walk away. And once I'd shown the stewardess the ring, she let me stay in club class until after take-off.' He picked it up, held it between his thumb and finger. 'Will you marry me, Louise?'

'A beach bum?' she said. Then, laughing, 'You are such a liar, Max Valentine.' But she held out her left hand, allowed him to slip the ring onto her finger. Kiss her.

'Shall we get married in Queensland?' he asked.

'I'm not going to Queensland. I'm going to Melbourne to open my Australian office,' she reminded him.

'Yes, I saw your little goodbye note in the *Courier*, but I'm going to Queensland. I've been given a lead on a fabulous new resort opening up there. Rainforest. The barrier reef. A marina…'

'Sounds wonderful.'

'So come and give me your opinion. Then I'll help you set up your own empire if that's still what you want.'

'Mmm. Maybe I should think about that. As a partner in Bella Lucia, I'm going to have other responsibilities.'

'As my wife, the mother of my children and a partner in Bella Lucia, you may have a point.'

'As my husband and the father of my children, you're going to be pretty busy yourself.'

'So, we have a deal?'

'No, we have a partnership, but forget the quiet wedding, Max. This time you have to turn up and face the music, a full dress occasion with a dozen bridesmaids, emotional family members and enough rose petals to scent all of Richmond Hill. She grinned. 'Do you think you can manage that?'

'Wild horses wouldn't keep me away.'

'Well, just in case you need reminding,' she said, unfastening a tiny gold pin from under the collar of her jacket, transferring it to his, 'you'd better have this. Don't lose it again.'

Louise was driven to her wedding in a ribbon-bedecked open carriage drawn by two white horses, her father at her side.

At the church gate, she was met with a barrage of photographers eager to get pictures of the high-society guests, of the bride herself. Inside the church porch, Jodie, who'd flown over for the wedding to be her matron of honour, was waiting to straighten her veil and train.

She had the bright nosegay of tiny bridesmaids, the daughters of Bella Lucia staff, each wearing a dress a different shade of pink from palest rose to darkest fuchsia, as well as two distinctly unimpressed page boys, firmly in hand and they all fell in behind the bride and her father without a fuss.

'The groom did manage to turn up, then?' John Valentine asked the verger.

'Oh, very eager, sir. First to arrive. I always think that's a good sign.'

'Hmmph. Well, yes, I'm sure you're right.'

Louise smiled behind her veil. She hadn't doubted Max, not for one moment. It wasn't that he never missed a date, but these days he never failed to phone and let her know if he was having a problem. If he'd be late.

'Ready?' the verger asked.

'Ready,' Louise assured him. 'And just as eager as the groom.'

A signal was given and as the first notes of the Wedding March reached them she leaned against her father just for a moment and said, 'You have been the best father a girl could ever have. Thank you.'

For once lost for words, he just squeezed her hand

in reply, tucked it beneath his arm before setting off with her up the aisle.

The church was full, not just with their parents, but crammed with Valentines from all over the world. Rachel, Luc and their baby, Rebecca, Mitch and their children, Emma, Queen of Meridia, with her king, Melissa, who had eyes for no one but her sultan, thanks, it appeared, to a little help from Max, Jack with Maddie, Beverley. Daniel and Stephanie, and Dominic with his wife and children. Patsy and Derek were there somewhere, too, but Louise saw only one man. Not even his best friend, Sheikh Surum Al-Thani of Qu'Arim, in all his robes, standing at Max's side, could eclipse the joy shining from the vivid blue eyes of the man she had loved all her life. From this day forward they were to be together for always. Partners. Lovers. Friends. Husband and wife.

As she reached him he smiled, took her hand, raised it to his lips and a soft sigh rippled through the church. Then they turned to face the vicar and the service began.

'Dearly beloved…'

Only when the vicar asked, 'Who giveth this Woman to be married to this Man?' was there the lightest hiccup in the service. Instead of simply putting her hand into Max's, her father said, quite distinctly, 'Me. I do…'

Afterwards, in the vestry as they signed the register her mother scolded him, but he was unrepentant. 'I just wanted Max to know,' he said. 'I wanted everyone to know that I'm happy.' He turned to his brother, put his hand on his shoulder. 'Really happy. It's a wonderful day.'

Max and Louise stood at the head of the receiving line, to greet their guests as they arrived for the reception. The guest list of family and friends read like an international Who's Who. They had come from Australia, America, France, Meridia, Qu'Arim. Old family from Italy mingled with Ivy's aristocratic relations.

And there was Patsy.

She came in last with her new husband and Louise kissed them both, then turned to her mother and said, 'Mum, may I introduce Patsy Simpson Harcourt and her husband Derek. Patsy, this is my mother.'

For a moment both women seemed frozen, then Ivy Valentine stepped forward, put her arms around Patsy and said, 'Thank you. Thank you, Patsy, for giving me the most wonderful daughter any woman could ever ask for.'

Louise might have cried, but at that moment Jack tapped a spoon against a champagne glass and said 'We're going to have the best afternoon and evening of our lives here, but before we get started I war us all to raise a glass in memory of William Valentine, who opened the first Bella Lucia restaurant sixty years ago and without whom we wouldn't be here today.'

A murmur of assent ran around the room.

'With Max and Louise now in charge the future is assured, so a toast to William Valentine and the great family he founded, to Bella Lucia. And to the next sixty years.'

'Sixty years?' Max looked adoringly at his bride. 'Are you game for that, my Valentine?'

'To be honest, I'm not into these short-term relationships,' she said, with an impish smile. 'But ask me again in sixty years. I'll give you my answer then.'

MILLS & BOON® PUBLISH EIGHT LARGE PRINT TITLES A MONTH. THESE ARE THE EIGHT TITLES FOR JUNE 2007.

TAKEN BY THE SHEIKH
Penny Jordan

THE GREEK'S VIRGIN
Trish Morey

THE FORCED BRIDE
Sara Craven

BEDDED AND WEDDED FOR REVENGE
Melanie Milburne

RANCHER AND PROTECTOR
Judy Christenberry

THE VALENTINE BRIDE
Liz Fielding

ONE SUMMER IN ITALY...
Lucy Gordon

CROWNED: AN ORDINARY GIRL
Natasha Oakley

MILLS & BOON®

MILLS & BOON PUBLISH EIGHT LARGE PRINT TITLES A MONTH. THESE ARE THE EIGHT TITLES FOR JULY 2007.

ROYALLY BEDDED, REGALLY WEDDED
Julia James

THE SHEIKH'S ENGLISH BRIDE
Sharon Kendrick

CILIAN HUSBAND, BLACKMAILED BRIDE
Kate Walker

AT THE GREEK BOSS'S BIDDING
Jane Porter

CATTLE RANCHER, CONVENIENT WIFE
Margaret Way

BAREFOOT BRIDE
Jessica Hart

THEIR VERY SPECIAL GIFT
Jackie Braun

HER PARENTHOOD ASSIGNMENT
Fiona Harper

MILLS & BOON®

0607 Rom LP